Nora Roberts is the number one *New York Times* bestseller of more than 200 novels. With over 500 million copies of her books in print, she is indisputably one of the most celebrated and popular writers in the world. She is both a *Sunday Times* bestseller in the UK and a number one bestseller in Australia.

By Nora Roberts

Many of Nora Roberts' other titles are now available in eBook and she is also the author of the In Death series using the pseudonym J.D. Robb.

NORA ROBERTS

REFLECTIONS

PIATKUS

PIATKUS

First published in the US in 1983 by Silhouette Books,
a division of Harlequin Books
First published in ebook in Great Britain in 2013 by Piatkus
This paperback edition published in 2021

1 3 5 7 9 10 8 6 4 2

A CIP catalogue record for this book
is available from the British Library.

ISBN 978-0-349-42708-9

Printed and bound in Great Britain by Clays Ltd, Elcograf S.p.A.

Papers used by Piatkus are from well-managed forests
and other responsible sources.

MIX
Paper from
responsible sources
FSC® C104740

Piatkus
An imprint of
Little, Brown Book Group
Carmelite House
50 Victoria Embankment
London EC4Y 0DZ

An Hachette UK Company
www.hachette.co.uk

www.littlebrown.co.uk

Chapter 1

The wind had cooled the air. It blew dark clouds across the sky and whistled through the leaves, now hinting at fall. Along the roadside the trees appeared more yellow than green, and touches of flame and scarlet were beginning to show. The day was poised in September, just as summer was turning autumn. The late afternoon sunshine squeezed between the clouds, slanting onto the roadway.

The air smelled of rain. Lindsay walked swiftly, knowing the clouds could win out at any moment. The breeze lifted and tossed the strands of her silvery blond hair, and she pushed at them with annoyance. She would have been wiser to have left it neatly pinned at the nape of her neck, she thought.

Had she not been so pressed for time, Lindsay would have enjoyed the walk. She would have reveled at the hint of fall and the threatening storm. Now, however, she hurried along the roadway wondering what else could go wrong.

In the three years since she had returned to Connecticut to teach, she had experienced some rough moments. But this, she decided, was among the top ten for frustration value. Backed up plumbing in the studio, a forty-five minute lecture from an overeager parent on her child's prowess, two torn costumes and a student with an upset stomach—these minor annoyances had culminated with her temperamental car. It had coughed and moaned as usual when she had turned the ignition, but then it had failed to pull itself together. It simply had sat there shuddering until Lindsay had admitted defeat. This car, she thought with a rueful smile, is about as old as I am, and we're both tired.

After taking a hopeless look under the hood, Lindsay had gritted her teeth and begun the two-and-a-half-mile hike home from the studio.

Of course, she admitted as she trudged along under the shifting sunlight, she could have called someone. She sighed, knowing her temper had set her off. Ten minutes of brisk walking had cooled it. Nerves, she told herself. I'm just nervous about the recital tonight. Not the recital, technically, she corrected, stuffing her hands into her pockets. The girls are ready; rehearsals had been perfect. The little ones are cute enough that mistakes won't matter. It was the times before and after the recitals that distressed Lindsay. And the parents.

She knew that some would be dissatisfied with their children's parts. And more still who would try to pressure her into accelerating the training. Why wasn't their Pavlova on *pointe* yet? Why did Mrs. Jones's ballerina have a bigger part than Mrs. Smith's? Shouldn't Sue move on to the intermediate class?

So often Lindsay's explanations on anatomy, growing bones, endurance and timing met with only more suggestions. Normally, she used a mixture of flattery, stubbornness and intimidation to hold them off. She prided herself on being able to handle overzealous parents. After all, she mused, hadn't her mother been exactly the same?

2

Above all else, Mae Dunne had wanted to see her daughter on stage. She herself was short-legged, with a small, compact body. But she had possessed the soul of a dancer. Through sheer determination and training, she had secured a place in the *corps de ballet* with a small touring company.

Mae had been nearly thirty when she married. Resigned that she would never be a principal dancer, she had turned to teaching for a short time, but her own frustrations made her a poor instructor. Lindsay's birth had altered everything. She could never be a prima ballerina, but her daughter would.

Lessons for Lindsay had begun at age five with Mae in constant attendance. From that time on, her life had been a flurry of lessons, recitals, ballet shoes and classical music. Her diet had been scrupulously monitored, her height agonized over until it was certain that five-feet-two was all she would achieve. Mae had been pleased. Toe shoes add six inches to a dancer's height, and a tall ballerina has a more difficult time finding partners.

Lindsay had inherited her mother's height, but to Mae's pride, her body was slender and delicate. After a brief, awkward stage, Lindsay had emerged as a teenager with fawnlike beauty: fragile blond hair, ivory skin, and Viking blue eyes with brows thin and naturally arched. Her bone structure was elegant, masking a sturdy strength gained from years of training. Her arms and legs were slim with the long muscles of a classical dancer. All of Mae's prayers had been answered.

Lindsay looked the part of a ballerina, and she had the talent. Mae didn't need a teacher to confirm what she could see for herself. There were the coordination, the technique, the endurance and the ability. But more, there was the heart.

At eighteen Lindsay had been accepted into a New York company.

Unlike her mother, she did not remain in the *corps*. She advanced to soloist, then, the year she turned twenty, she became a principal dancer. For nearly two years it seemed that Mae's dreams were reality. Then, without warning, Lindsay had been forced to give up her position and return to Connecticut.

For three years teaching dance had been her profession. Though Mae was bitter, Lindsay was more philosophical. She was a dancer still. That would never change.

The clouds shifted again to block out the sun. Lindsay shivered and wished she had remembered her jacket. It sat in the front seat of her car, where, in the heat of her temper, she had tossed it. Her arms were now bare, covered only at the shoulders by a pale blue leotard. She had pulled on jeans, and her leg-warmers helped, but she thought longingly of the jacket. Because thinking of it failed to warm her, Lindsay quickened her pace to a jog. Her muscles responded instantly. There was a fluidity to the motion, a grace instinctive rather than planned. She began to enjoy the run. It was her nature to hunt for pleasure and to find it.

Abruptly, as if a hand had pulled the plug, the rain began. Lindsay stopped to stare up at the churning, black sky. "What else?" she demanded. A deep roar of thunder answered her. With a half-laugh, she shook her head. The Moorefield house was just across the street. She decided to do what she should have done initially: ask Andy to drive her home. Hugging her arms, she stepped out into the road.

The rude blast of a horn had her heart bounding to her throat. Her head snapped around, and she made out the dim shape of a car approaching through the curtain of rain. Instantly she leaped out of the way, slipping on the wet pavement and landing with a splash in a shallow puddle.

Lindsay shut her eyes as her pulse quickened. She heard the high squeal of brakes and the skid of tires. Years from now, she thought as the cold wetness soaked through her jeans, I'll laugh at this. But not now. She kicked and sent a small spray of water flying.

"Are you out of your mind?"

Lindsay heard the roar through the rain and opened her eyes. Standing over her was a raging, wet giant. Or a devil, she thought, eyeing him warily as he towered over her. He was dressed in black. His hair was black as well; sleek and wet, it enhanced a tanned, raw-boned face. There was something faintly wicked about that face. Perhaps it was the dark brows that rose ever so slightly at the ends. Perhaps it was the strange contrast of his eyes, a pale green that brought the sea to mind. And at the moment, they were furious. His nose was long and rather sharp, adding to the angular impression of his face. His clothes were plastered against his body by the rain and revealed a firm, well-proportioned frame. Had she not been so absorbed with his face, Lindsay would have admired it profession-ally. Speechless, she only stared up at him, her eyes huge.

"Are you hurt?" he demanded when she failed to answer his first question. There was no concern in his voice, only restrained anger. Lindsay shook her head and continued to stare. With an impatient oath, he took her arms and pulled her up, lifting her well off the ground before he set her on her feet. "Don't you look where you're going?" he tossed out, giving her a quick shake before releasing her.

He was not the giant Lindsay had first imagined. He was tall, cer-tainly—perhaps a foot taller than herself—but hardly a bone-crushing giant or satanic apparition. She began to feel more foolish than frightened.

"I'm terribly sorry," she began. She was fully aware that she had been at fault and equally willing to admit it. "I did look, but I didn't…"

5

"Looked?" he interrupted. The impatience in his tone barely covered a deeper, tightly controlled fury. "Then perhaps you'd better start wearing your glasses. I'm sure your father paid good money for them."

Lightning flashed once, slicing white across the sky. More than the words, Lindsay resented the tone. "I don't wear glasses," she retorted.

"Then perhaps you should."

"My eyes are fine." She pushed clinging hair from her brow.

"Then you certainly should know better than to walk out into the middle of the street."

Rain streamed down her face as she glared at him. She wondered that it didn't turn to steam. "I apologized," she snapped, placing her hands on her hips. "Or had begun to before you jumped on me. If you expect groveling, you can forget it. If you hadn't been so heavy on the horn, I wouldn't have slipped and landed in that stupid puddle." She wiped ineffectually at the seat of her pants. "I don't suppose it occurs to you to apologize?"

"No," he answered evenly, "it doesn't. I'm hardly responsible for your clumsiness."

"Clumsiness?" Lindsay repeated. Her eyes grew round and wide. *"Clumsiness?"* On the repetition, her voice broke. To her, there was no insult more vile. *"How dare you!"*

She would take the dunk in the puddle, she would take his rudeness, but she would not take that. "You're the most deplorable excuse for a man I've ever met!" Her face was aglow with passion now, and she pushed impatiently at the hair the rain continued to nudge into her eyes. They shone an impossibly vivid blue against her flushed skin. "You nearly run me down, frighten me to death, push me into a puddle, lecture me as if I were a near-sighted child and now, *now* you have the nerve to call me *clumsy!"*

A winglike brow raised up at the passion of her speech. "If the shoe fits," he murmured, then stunned her by grabbing her arm and pulling her with him.

"Just what are you doing?" Lindsay demanded, trying for imperviousness and ending on a squeak.

"Getting out of this damn downpour." He opened the car door on the driver's side and shoved her, without ceremony, inside. Automatically, Lindsay scooted across the seat to accommodate him. "I can hardly leave you out in the rain." His tone was brusque as he moved in beside her at the wheel and slammed the door behind him. The storm battered against the windows.

He dragged his fingers through the thick hank of hair that was now plastered against his forehead, and Lindsay was immediately taken with his hand. It had the wide palm and long-fingered extension of a pianist. She almost felt sympathy for his predicament. But then he turned his head. The look was enough to erase any empathy.

"Where were you going?" he asked. The question was curt, as though it had been put to a child. Lindsay straightened her wet, chilled shoulders.

"Home, about a mile straight down this road."

The brows lifted again as he took a good, long look at her. Her hair hung limp and straight around her face. Her lashes were darkened and curled without the aid of mascara, framing eyes almost shockingly blue. Her mouth pouted, but it obviously did not belong to the child he had first taken her for. Though unpainted, it was clearly a woman's mouth. The naked face had something beyond simple beauty, but before he could define it, Lindsay shivered, distracting him.

"If you're going to go out in the rain," he said mildly as he reached toward the back seat, "you should take care to dress for it." He tossed a tan jacket into her lap.

7

"I don't need…" Lindsay began, only to break off by sneezing twice. Teeth clenched, she slipped her arms into the jacket as he started the engine. They drove in silence with the rain drumming on the roof.

It occurred to Lindsay all at once that the man was a total stranger. She knew virtually everyone in the small seacoast town by name or by sight, but never had she seen this man. She would hardly have forgotten that face. It was easy, in the slow-moving, friendly atmosphere of Cliffside, to be casual, but Lindsay had also spent several years in New York. She knew the very real dangers of accepting rides from strangers. Surreptitiously, she inched closer to the passenger door.

"A bit late to think of that now," he said quietly.

Lindsay's head snapped around. She thought, but couldn't be certain, that his mouth lifted slightly at the corner. She angled her chin. "Just there," she said coolly, pointing to the left. "The cedar house with the dormers."

The car purred to a halt in front of a white picket fence. Pulling together all her dignity, Lindsay turned to him again. She fully intended to make her thanks frosty.

"You'd better get out of those wet clothes," he advised before she could speak. "And next time, look both ways before you cross the street."

She could only make a strangled sound of fury as she fumbled for the door handle. Stepping back into the torrent of rain, she glared across the seat. "Thanks heaps," she snapped and slammed the door peevishly. She dashed around the back of the car and through the gate, forgetting she still wore a stranger's jacket.

Lindsay stormed into the house. With her temper still simmering, she stood quite still, eyes shut, calling herself to order. The incident had been infuriating, outrageously so, but the last thing she wanted was to have to relate the entire story to her mother. Lindsay was aware that her face was too expressive, her eyes too revealing. Her tendency to so visibly express her feelings had been only another asset in her career. When she danced *Giselle,* she felt as Giselle. The audience could read the tragedy on Lindsay's face. When she danced, she became utterly rapt in the story and in the music. But when her ballet shoes came off and she was Lindsay Dunne again, she knew it was not wise to let her thoughts shout from her eyes.

If she saw that Lindsay was upset, Mae would question her and demand a detailed account, only to criticize in the end. At the moment, the last thing that Lindsay wanted was a lecture. Wet and tired, she wearily began to climb the stairs to the second floor. It was then that she heard the slow, uneven footsteps, a constant reminder of the accident that had killed Lindsay's father.

"Hi! I was just dashing upstairs to change." Lindsay pulled back the wet hair from her face to smile at her mother, who stood at the foot of the stairs. Mae rested her hand on the newel post. Though her carefully coiffed hair had been dyed an ageless blond and her makeup had been skillfully applied, the effect was spoiled by Mae's perpetual expression of dissatisfaction.

"The car was acting up," Lindsay continued before the questioning could begin. "I got caught in the rain before I got a lift. Andy will have to give me a ride back tonight," she added in afterthought.

"You forgot to give him back his jacket," Mae observed. She leaned heavily on the newel post as she looked at her daughter. The damp weather plagued her hip.

"Jacket?" Blankly, Lindsay looked down and saw the wet, too-long sleeves that hung over her arms. "Oh no!"

"Well, don't look so panic-stricken," Mae said testily as she shifted her weight. "Andy can manage without it until tonight."

9

"Andy?" Lindsay repeated, then made the connection her mother had guessed at. Explanations, she decided, were too complicated. "I suppose so," she agreed casually. Then, descending a step, she laid her hand over her mother's. "You look tired, Mother. Did you rest today?"

"Don't treat me like a child," Mae snapped, and Lindsay immediately stiffened. She drew her hand away.

"I'm sorry." Her tone was restrained, but hurt flickered into her eyes. "I'll just go up and change before dinner." She would have turned, but Mae caught at her arm.

"Lindsay." She sighed, easily reading the emotions in the wide, blue eyes. "I'm sorry; I'm bad-tempered today. The rain depresses me."

"I know." Lindsay's voice softened. It had been a combination of rain and poor tires that had caused her parents' accident.

"And I hate your staying here taking care of me when you should be in New York."

"Mother..."

"It's no use." Mae's voice was sharp again. "Things won't be right until you're where you belong, where you're meant to be." Mae turned, moving down the hall in her awkward, uneven gate.

Lindsay watched her disappear before she turned to mount the stairs. Where I belong, she mused as she turned into her room. Where is that really? Closing the door, she leaned back against it.

The room was big and airy with two wide windows side by side. On the dresser that had been her grandmother's was a collection of shells gathered from a beach barely a mile from the house. Set in a corner was a shelf stacked with books from her childhood. The faded Oriental rug was a prize she had brought back with her when she had closed up her New York apartment. The rocking chair was from the flea market two blocks away, and the framed Renoir print was from a Manhattan art gallery. Her room, she thought, reflected the two worlds in which she had lived.

Over the bed hung the pale pink toe shoes she had worn in her first professional solo. Lindsay walked over to them and lightly fingered the satin ribbons. She remembered sewing them on, remembered the stomach-churning excitement. She remembered her mother's ecstatic face after the performance and her father's gently awed one.

A lifetime ago, she thought as she let the satin fall from her fingers. Back then she had believed that anything was possible. Perhaps, for a time, it had been.

Smiling, Lindsay let herself remember the music, the movement, the magic and the times she had felt her body was without bounds, fluid and free. Reality had come afterward, with unspeakable cramping, bleeding feet, strained muscles. How had it been possible, again and again, to contort her body into the unnatural lines that made up the dance? But she had done it, and she had pushed herself to the limits of ability and endurance. She had given herself over, sacrificing her body and the years. There had been only the dance. It had absorbed her utterly.

Shaking her head, Lindsay brought herself back. That, she reminded herself, was a long time ago. Now, she had other things to think about. She stripped out of the damp jacket, then frowned at it. What do I do with this? she wondered.

The owner's blatant rudeness came back to her. Her frown deepened. Well, if he wants it, he can just come back for it. A quick scan of the material and the label told her it was not a piece of clothing to be carelessly forgotten. But the mistake was hardly her fault, she told herself as she walked to the closet for a hanger. If he hadn't made her so mad, she wouldn't have forgotten to give it back to him.

She hung the jacket in her closet and began to peel off her own wet clothes. She slipped a thick, chenille robe over her shivering skin and closed the closet doors. She told herself to forget the jacket and the man it belonged to. Neither of them, she decided, had anything to do with her.

Chapter 2

It was a different Lindsay Dunne who stood greeting parents two hours later. She wore a high-necked, ruffled lawn blouse with a full, knife-pleated skirt, both in a rain-washed shade of blue. Her hair was neatly braided and coiled at each ear. Her features were calm and composed. Any resemblance to the wet, furious woman of the early evening had vanished. In her preoccupation with the recital, Lindsay had completely forgotten the incident in the rain.

Chairs had been set up in rows from which parents could watch their children's performance. Behind the audience was a table on which coffee and assorted cookies had been arranged. Throughout the room Lindsay could hear the buzz of conversation, and it made her recall the innumerable recitals of her own past. She tried not to hurry through the handshakings and questions, but her mind flitted to the adjoining room, where two dozen girls were busy with tutus and toe shoes.

She was nervous. Underneath the calm, smiling exterior, Lindsay was every bit as nervous as she had been before every one of her own recitals. But she managed to field questions smoothly, knowing almost invariably in advance what they would be. She'd been here before, as a preschooler, a junior, an intermediate and as a senior dancer. Now she was the instructor. Lindsay felt there was no aspect of a recital that she had missed in her lifetime. Yet she was still nervous.

The quiet Beethoven sonata she had placed on the CD player had been an attempt to quiet her own nerves as much as to create atmosphere. It was foolish, she told herself, for a seasoned professional— an established instructor—to be nervous and tense over a simple recital. But there was no help for it. Lindsay's heart was very close to the surface when it came to her school and her students. She wanted badly for the evening to be a success.

She smiled, shaking hands with a father whom she was certain would rather be at home watching a ball game. The finger he eased surreptitiously under his collar made it plain that he was uncomfortable in the restricting tie. If Lindsay had known him better, she would have laughed, then whispered to him to remove it.

Since she had started giving recitals more than two years before, one of Lindsay's main objectives had been to keep the parents at ease. Her rule of thumb was that comfortable parents made a more enthusiastic audience, and a more enthusiastic audience could generate more students for the school. She had founded the school by word of mouth, and it was still a neighbor's recommendation to a neighbor, a satisfied parent's suggestion to an acquaintance, that kept it working. It was her business now, her living as well as her love. She considered herself fortunate to have been able to combine the two for a second time in her life.

Aware that many of the dancers' families had come out of a sense of duty, Lindsay was determined to give them a good time. In each recital, she tried not only to vary the program but to see to it that every dancer had a part especially choreographed for her talent and

14

ability. She knew that not all mothers were as ambitious for their children as Mae, nor were all fathers as supportive as hers had been.

But they came anyway, she thought, looking around her at the group huddled in her studio. They drove out in the rain, giving up a favorite television show or an after-dinner snooze on the sofa. Lindsay smiled, touched again by the perpetually unnoticed selfless-ness of parents dealing with their children.

It struck her then—strongly, as it did from time to time—how very glad she was to have come home, how very content she was to remain here. Oh, she had loved New York, the continual throb of life, the demands, the undeniable excitement, but the simple pleasure of the close-knit town and the quiet streets more than satisfied her now.

Everyone in the room knew each other, either by sight or by name. The mother of one of the senior dancers had been Lindsay's sitter almost twenty years before. She'd worn a ponytail then, Lindsay remembered as she looked at the woman's short, sculp-tured hairstyle. It had been a long ponytail tied up with colored yarn. It had swung when she walked, and Lindsay had found it beautiful. Now the memory warmed her and eased her nerves.

Perhaps everyone should leave at some point, then come back to their hometown as an adult, she reflected, whether they settled down there again or not. What a revelation it is to see the things and people we knew as children through an adult's perspective.

"Lindsay."

Lindsay turned to greet a former schoolmate, now the mother of one of her smallest dancers. "Hello, Jackie. You look wonderful."

Jackie was a trim and competent brunette. Lindsay recalled that she had been on an amazing number of committees during their high school years. "We're awfully nervous," Jackie confessed, referring to herself, her daughter and her husband as one.

15

Lindsay followed Jackie's eyes across the room and spotted the former track star turned insurance executive whom Jackie had married within a year of graduation. He was talking with two elderly couples. All the grandparents are here as well, Lindsay thought with a smile.

"You're supposed to be nervous," Lindsay told her. "It's traditional."

"I hope she'll do well," Jackie said, "for her sake. And she wants so badly to impress her daddy."

"She'll be just fine," Lindsay assured her, giving the nervous hand a squeeze. "And they'll all look wonderful, thanks to the help you gave me with the costumes. I haven't had a chance to thank you yet."

"Oh, that was a pleasure," Jackie assured her. She glanced toward her family again. "Grandparents," she said in an undertone, "can be terrifying."

Lindsay laughed softly, knowing how these particular grandparents doted on the tiny dancer.

"Go ahead, laugh," Jackie invited scornfully, but a self-deprecating smile touched her lips. "You don't have to worry about grandparents yet. Or in-laws," she added, giving the word a purposefully ominous tone. "By the way," Jackie's change of tone put Lindsay on immediate alert. "My cousin Tod...you remember?"

"Yes," Lindsay answered cautiously as Jackie paused.

"He's coming through town in a couple of weeks. Just for a day or so." She gave Lindsay a guileless smile. "He asked about you the last time he phoned."

"Jackie..." Lindsay began, determined to be firm.

"Why don't you let him take you out to dinner?" Jackie continued, cutting off Lindsay's chance to make a clean escape. "He was so taken with you last year. He'll only be in town for a short time. He has a

16

marvellous business in New Hampshire. You know, hardware; I told you."

"I remember," Lindsay said rather shortly. One of the disadvantages of being single in a small town was continually having to dodge matchmaking schemes by well-meaning friends, she thought. The hints and suggestions for partners had been dropped more frequently now that Mae was improving steadily. Lindsay knew that in order to avoid a deluge, she must set a precedent. She must be firm.

"Jackie, you know how busy I am…."

"You're doing a wonderful job here, Lindsay," Jackie said quickly. "The girls all love you, but a woman needs a diversion now and then, doesn't she? There's nothing serious between you and Andy?"

"No, of course not, but…"

"Then there certainly isn't any need to bury yourself."

"My mother…"

"She looked so well when I dropped off the costumes at your house the other day," Jackie went on relentlessly. "It was wonderful to see her up and around. She's finally putting on a bit of weight, I noticed."

"Yes, she is, but…"

"Tod should be in town a week from Thursday. I'll tell him to give you a ring," Jackie said lightly before turning to weave her way through the crowd to her family.

Lindsay watched her retreat with a mixture of irritation and amusement. Never expect to win over someone who won't let you finish a sentence, she concluded. Oh well, she thought, one cousin with a nervous voice and slightly damp palms won't be too bad for an evening. Her social calendar wasn't exactly bulging with appointments, and fascinating men weren't exactly lining up at her front door.

Lindsay pushed the prospective dinner date to the back of her mind. Now wasn't the time to worry about it. Now was the time to think of her students. She walked across the studio to the dressing room. Here, at least, her authority was absolute.

Once inside, she leaned back against the closed door and took a long, deep breath. Before her, pandemonium ruled, but this was the sort of chaos she was immune to. Girls chattered excitedly, helping each other into costumes or trying out steps one final time. One senior dancer calmly executed *pliés* while a pair of five-year-olds played tug of war with a ballet shoe. All around there was the universal backstage confusion.

Lindsay straightened, her voice rising with the gesture. "I'd like your attention, please." The soft tone carried over the chattering and brought all eyes to her.

"We'll begin in ten minutes. Beth, Josey," she addressed two senior dancers with a nod, "if you'd help the little ones." Lindsay glanced at her watch, wondering why the piano accompanist was so late. If worse comes to worst, she would use the CD player.

She crouched to adjust the tights on a young student and dealt with questions and nerves from others.

"Ms. Dunne, you didn't let my brother sit in the front row, did you? He makes faces. Awful ones."

"Second row from the back," Lindsay countered with a mouthful of hairpins as she completed repairs on a tousled coiffure.

"Ms. Dunne, I'm worried about the second set of *jetés*."

"Just like rehearsal. You'll be wonderful."

"Ms. Dunne, Kate's wearing red nail polish."

"Hmm." Lindsay glanced at her watch again.

"Ms. Dunne, about the *fouettés*…"

"Five, no more."

"We really ought to be wearing stage makeup so we don't look washed out," a diminutive dancer complained.

"No," Lindsay said flatly, suppressing a smile. "Monica, thank goodness!" Lindsay suddenly called out with relief as an attractive young woman entered through the back door. "I was about to drag out the CD player."

"Sorry I'm late." Monica grinned cheerfully as she shut the door at her back.

Monica Anderson at twenty was pretty in a healthy, wholesome way. Her bouncy blond hair adorned a face that featured a dash of freckles and large, hopeful, brown eyes. She had a tall, athletic body and the purest heart of anyone Lindsay had ever known. She collected stray cats, listened to both sides of every argument and never thought the worst of anyone, even after being confronted with it. Lindsay liked her for her simple goodness.

Monica also possessed a true gift for piano accompaniment. She kept tempo, playing the classics truthfully, without the embellishments that would detract from the dancers. But she was not, Lindsay thought with a sigh, overly obsessed with punctuality.

"We've got about five minutes," Lindsay reminded her as Monica maneuvered her generously curved body toward the door.

"No problem. I'll go out in just a second. This is Ruth," she continued, gesturing to a girl who stood just to the side of the door. "She's a dancer."

Lindsay's attention shifted from the tall, busty blonde to the finely boned girl. She noted the exotic, almond-shaped eyes and the full, passionate mouth. Ruth's straight, black hair was parted in the center to frame her small, triangular face and hung down just past her shoulder blades. Her features were uneven, and while individually they might have been unremarkable, in combination they were arresting. She was a girl on the brink of womanhood. Though her stance was easy and full of confidence, there was something in the dark eyes that bespoke uncertainty and nervousness. The eyes caused Lindsay's smile to warm as she held out her hand.

"Hello, Ruth."

"I'll go give them a quick overture and quiet things down," Monica interjected, but as she turned to go, Ruth plucked at her sleeve.

"But, Monica..." Ruth protested.

"Oh, Ruth wants to talk to you, Lindsay." She gave her cheerful, toothy smile and turned once more toward the door. "Don't worry," she said to the younger girl, "Lindsay's very nice. I told you. Ruth's a little nervous," she announced as she backed out the door leading to the studio.

Amused, Lindsay shook her head, but as she turned back, she saw Ruth's heightened color. At ease with strangers herself, she still recognized one who was not. She touched the girl's arm lightly. "There's only one Monica," she stated with a new smile. "Now, if you'll give me a hand lining up the first dancers, we should be able to talk."

"I don't want to be in the way, Ms. Dunne."

In answer, Lindsay gestured behind her to the backstage confusion. "I could use the help."

Lindsay was easily capable of organizing the dancers herself, but she knew, watching Ruth relax, that she had made the right gesture. Intrigued, she watched the way the girl moved, recognizing natural grace and trained style. Lindsay then turned to give her full attention to her students. In a few moments, a restrained hush fell over the room. After opening the door, she gave a quick signal to Monica. The introductory music began, then the youngest of Lindsay's students glided into the studio.

"They're so cute at this stage," she murmured. "There's very little they can do wrong." Already some of the pirouettes had touched off smatterings of applause. "Posture," she whispered to the small dancers. Then to Ruth: "How long have you been studying?"

"Since I was five."

Lindsay nodded while keeping her eyes trained on the tiny performers. "How old are you?"

"Seventeen."

It was stated with such determination that Lindsay lifted a brow.

"Just last month," Ruth added with a tinge of defense. Lindsay smiled but continued to watch the dancers.

"I was five, too. My mother still has my first pair of ballet shoes."

"I saw you dance in *Don Quixote*." The words tumbled out swiftly. Lindsay turned to see Ruth staring at her, her bottom lip trapped between her teeth.

"Did you? When?"

"Five years ago in New York. You were wonderful." The eyes were so filled with awe and admiration that Lindsay lifted a hand to the girl's cheek. Ruth stiffened, but Lindsay, puzzled, smiled nonetheless.

"Thank you. It was always my favorite ballet. So full of flash and fire."

"I'm going to dance Dulcinea one day." Some of the nerves had faded from the voice. Now Ruth's eyes were direct on Lindsay's.

Studying her, Lindsay thought she had never seen more perfect looks for the part. "Do you want to continue your training?"

"Yes." Ruth moistened her lips.

She tilted her head, still studying. "With me?"

Ruth nodded before the word would come. "Yes."

"Tomorrow's Saturday." Lindsay lifted her hand to signal the next group of dancers. "My first class is at ten. Can you come at nine?"

The triumphant preschoolers forged back into the dressing room. "I'll want to check the progress of your training to see where to place you. Bring ballet and toe shoes."

Ruth's eyes shimmered with excitement. "Yes, Ms. Dunne. Nine o'clock."

"I'd also like to speak with your parents, Ruth, if one or both of them could come with you."

Monica changed tempo to introduce the next group.

"My parents were killed in an accident a few months ago."

Lindsay heard the quiet pronouncement as she nudged the next group out on stage. Over their heads, her eyes met Ruth's. She saw that the light in them had dimmed. "Oh, Ruth, I'm terribly sorry." Sympathy and distress deepened Lindsay's tone. She knew the feel of tragedy. But Ruth shook her head briskly and avoided the touch of her hand. Suppressing the instinctive need to comfort, Lindsay stood silently while Ruth composed herself. She recognized a very private person, one who was not yet ready to share her emotions.

"I live with my uncle," Ruth continued. There was nothing of her feelings in her voice. It was low and smooth. "We've just moved into the house on the edge of town."

"The Cliff House." Fresh interest sparkled in Lindsay's eyes. "I'd heard it'd been sold. It's a fabulous place." Ruth merely looked off into space. She hates it, Lindsay decided, again feeling a profound tug of sympathy. She hates everything about it. It was difficult to keep her tone practical. "Well, then, perhaps your uncle could come in with you. If it's not convenient, have him phone me. I'm in the book. It's important that I speak with him before we outline your routine."

A sudden smile illuminated Ruth's face. "Thank you, Ms. Dunne."

Lindsay turned away to quiet a pair of youngsters. When she looked again, Ruth had gone.

An odd girl, she mused, obliging one of the little ones by picking her up. *Lonely.* The word seemed too suitable, and Lindsay nuzzled against the neck of the small child she held. She had had little time for loneliness, but she recognized it. It saddened her to see it reflected in the eyes of one so young.

She wondered what the uncle was like as she watched her intermediate students carry out a short routine from *Sleeping Beauty.* Is he kind? Is he understanding? She thought again of the large, dark eyes and sighed. Monica had found another stray, and Lindsay knew she had already involved herself. Smiling, she kissed the little ballerina's cheek, then set her down.

Tomorrow, Lindsay decided, we'll see if she can dance.

Lindsay began to wonder if the rain would last forever. It was warm—even cozy—in her bed, but the night wore on, and she was still wide awake. It was odd, she thought, because usually the patter of lingering rain and the soft quilt around her would have induced sleep. She thought perhaps it was leftover tension from the recital which kept her mind alert.

It had gone well, she recalled, pleased. The little ones, shaky posture and all, had been as appealing as she had hoped, and the older girls had demonstrated all the poise and grace she could have asked of them. If only she could lure some boys into class! She sighed. But she had to put that out of her mind. The recital had gone well, her students were happy. Some of them showed potential. But soon her thoughts drifted to the dark-haired girl, Ruth.

Lindsay had recognized ambition there but wondered if she would find talent. Remembering Ruth's eyes and the need and vulnerability she had seen there, she hoped she would. She wants to dance Dulcinea, she remembered with a wistful smile. Lindsay felt a small ache, knowing how many hopes could be dashed to the ground in the world of dance. She could only hope Ruth's weren't, for something in the young, poignant face had touched a chord in her. There had been a day not so long ago when dancing Dulcinea had been only a wish for Lindsay as well. She thought perhaps she had come full circle.

Lindsay closed her eyes, but her mind continued to race.

She briefly considered going down to the kitchen for some tea or hot chocolate. She sighed into the darkness. The noise would disturb her mother. Mae slept lightly, especially in the rain. Lindsay knew how difficult it was for her mother to deal with all the disappointments she had been handed. And the tragedy.

Mae's aching hip would be a continual reminder of the death of her husband. Lindsay knew that Mae had not always been happy, but her father had been so quietly supportive. His loss had been hard on Mae, who had awakened from a coma confused and in pain, unable to understand how he could have been taken from her. Lindsay knew her mother could never forget her husband's death, her own injuries and painful therapy and the abrupt end of her daughter's career.

And now that Mae was finally accepting Dad's death, Lindsay reflected, and could get around a bit more, she thought of nothing but Lindsay's return to professional dancing.

Lindsay rolled to her side, curling her arm under her pillow. The rain splashed on the window glass, excited by the wind. What would it take to resign her mother to the inevitable, she wondered. What would it take to make her happy? Would she ever be able to do both? The look on her mother's face as she had stood at the base of the stairs that afternoon came back to her. With the image came the familiar helplessness and guilt.

Rolling onto her back, Lindsay stared at the ceiling. She had to stop thinking about it. It was the rain, she decided, just the rain. To ease her insomnia, she began to go over the details of the day.

What an afternoon it had been. The varied complications now brought on a smile. Still, for a Friday class in which older girls were always thinking about their Saturday night dates and the younger ones were just thinking about Saturday, it had gone fairly well. And everything had worked out, except for that blasted car!

The thought of her broken-down car pushed the memory of the man in the rain back into Lindsay's mind. Frowning, she turned her head so that she faced the closet. In the near-perfect darkness, it was impossible to see the door itself, much less what was inside it. But Lindsay continued to frown. I wonder, she thought, if he'll come back for his jacket.

He had been so rude! Indignation welled up again, replacing her earlier depression. She much preferred it. He was so superior? *If you're going to go out in the rain...* In her mind she mimicked his low, controlled voice.

A wonderfully appealing voice, she reflected. Too bad it has to come out of such an unappealing man. Clumsy, she thought, fuming all over again. And he had the nerve to call me clumsy! She rolled onto her stomach and pounded the pillow before placing her head on it. I hope he does come back for his jacket, she decided. This time I'll be ready for him. It gave her a great deal of pleasure to imagine a variety of situations in which she returned the borrowed jacket. Haughtily, disdainfully, benevolently...she would hold the upper hand and humiliate the objectionable man whose eyes and cheekbones now haunted her. When next they met, it would not be raining. She would not be at a disadvantage—soaking wet and sneezing. She would be witty, poised...devastating. She smiled to herself as she drifted off to sleep.

Chapter 3

Rain had accumulated in puddles. The morning sun glistened on their surfaces in a splash of colors, while beads of moisture still clung to the grass. There was just a trace of fog misting over the ground. Andy turned up the car heater to combat the chill as he watched Lindsay walk through the front door of her house. She was, to him, the most gorgeous creature in the world. In point of fact, Andy felt Lindsay was beyond the real world. She was too delicate, too ethereal to be of the earth.

And her beauty was so pure, so fragile. It tied his stomach into knots when he saw her. It had been so for fifteen years.

Lindsay smiled and lifted a hand in greeting as she moved down the concrete walk toward the car. In her smile he saw the affection, the friendship she had always offered to him. Andy returned both the smile and the wave. He had no illusions about his relationship with Lindsay. Friendship and no more. It would never be anything else. Not once in all the time he had known her had she encouraged him beyond the borders of friendship.

She's not for me, Andy mused as Lindsay swung through the gate. But he felt the familiar surge when she opened the car door and slid in beside him. Her scent was always the same, light and fresh with a touch of the mysterious. He always felt too big when she was beside him. Too broad, too clumsy.

Lindsay smiled into his wide, square-jawed face and kissed him with quick friendliness. "Andy, you're a life-saver." She studied his face, liking it as always; the dependable dark eyes, the strong bones, the slightly disheveled brown hair reminiscent of a family dog. And like a family pet, he made her feel comfortable and just a little maternal. "I really appreciate your driving me to the studio this way."

He shrugged broad shoulders. Already the surge had mellowed into the familiar warmth he felt whenever she was near. "You know I don't mind."

"I know you don't," she acknowledged as he pulled away from the curb. "So I appreciate it even more." As was her habit, she slid sideways in the seat as she spoke. Personal contact was vital to her. "Your mom's coming by to spend some time with mine today."

"Yeah, I know." Andy drove down the street with the relaxed attention of one who had followed the same route uncountable times. "She's going to talk her into taking that trip to California this winter."

"I really hope she does." For a moment Lindsay allowed her mind to linger on her mother's restless, unhappy face. "She could use a change."

"How's she doing?"

Lindsay let out a long sigh. There was nothing she felt she could not discuss with Andy. She'd had no closer friend since childhood. "Physically, so much better. There's a great improvement even in the last three months, but otherwise..." She linked her fingers together, then turned her hands palms up, a gesture she used as others used a shrug. "Frustrated, angry, restless. She wants me to go back to New York to dance. She can't see it any other way. It's tunnel vision; she's

27

refused to accept the fact that picking up where I left off is virtually impossible. Three years away, three years older." She shook her head and lapsed into thoughtful silence. Andy gave her a full minute.

"Do you want to go back?"

She looked back at him now, and though the frown brought a line between her brows, it was one of concentration and not annoyance. "I don't know. I don't think so. I did it all once, and I'm very content here, but..." She sighed.

"But?" Andy turned left and absently waved to a pair of youngsters on bicycles.

"I loved it when I was doing it, even though so much of the life is brutal. I loved it." She smiled, relaxing against the seat again. "Past tense, you see. But Mother continually pushes it into the present. Even if I wanted it—wanted it desperately—the chance that the company would have me back is so—so slim." Her eyes wandered to the familiar houses. "So much of me belongs here now. It feels right, being home. Do you remember that night we snuck into the Cliff House?" Her eyes were alight again, laughing. Andy responded with a grin.

"I was scared to pieces. I still swear I saw the ghost."

Lindsay's laugh was a light, bubbling sound. "Ghost or no ghost, it's the most fantastic place I've ever seen. You know, it was finally sold."

"I'd heard." Andy shot her a look. "I remember you swearing you'd live there one day."

"We were young," she murmured, but the sadness she felt at the memory was warm and not unpleasant. "I wanted to live high up above the town and feel important. All those marvelous rooms stacked on top of each other, and those endless corridors," she recalled out loud.

"The place is a labyrinth," he remarked unromantically. "There's been a lot of work going on up there."

"I hope they haven't ruined the atmosphere."

"What, spider webs and field mice?"

Lindsay wrinkled her nose. "No, idiot, the stateliness, the magnificence, the arrogance. I've always imagined it with the gardens blooming and the windows wide open for parties."

"The place hasn't had a window open in more than a decade, and the garden has the toughest weeds in New England."

"You," she said gravely, "have no vision. Anyway," she continued, "the girl I'm seeing this morning is the niece of the man who bought the place. Know anything about him?"

"Nope. Mom might; she's always up on the town's latest gossip."

"I like the girl," Lindsay mused, conjuring up a picture of Ruth's poignant beauty. "She has rather a lost look. I'd like to help her."

"You think she needs help?"

"She seemed like a bird who wasn't quite certain whether the hand held out to her would squeeze or stroke. I wonder what the uncle's like."

Andy pulled into the studio parking lot. "How much could you find wrong with the man who bought the Cliff House?"

"Very little, I'm sure," she agreed, slamming her door behind her as Andy slammed his.

"I'll take a look at your car," he volunteered, and moving to it, lifted the hood. Lindsay walked to stand beside him. She scowled at the engine.

"It looks dreadful in there."

"It might help if you'd have it serviced once in a while." He grimaced at the grime-coated engine, then gave a disgusted look at the spark plugs. "You know, there are things that need to be replaced other than gas."

"I'm a mechanical failure," Lindsay said carelessly.

"You don't have to be a mechanic to take minimal care of a car," Andy began, and Lindsay groaned.

"A lecture. It's better to plead guilty." She threw her arms around his neck and kissed both his cheeks. "I'm incompetent. Forgive me."

Lindsay watched the grin flash just as she heard another car pull into the lot. With her arms still around Andy's neck, she turned her head. "That must be Ruth," she thought aloud before releasing him. "I really appreciate your checking out the car, Andy. If it's anything terminal, try to break it to me gently."

Turning around to greet Ruth, Lindsay was struck dumb. The man who approached with the girl was tall and dark. Lindsay knew how his voice would sound before he spoke. Just as she knew his taste in jackets.

"Marvelous," she said just under her breath. Their eyes locked. She decided he was not a man who surprised easily.

"Ms. Dunne?" There was a hesitant question in Ruth's voice. Shock, distress and annoyance were all easily read on Lindsay's face. "You did say I should be here at nine?"

"What?" Lindsay stared a moment. "Oh, yes," she said quickly. "I'm sorry. I've had some car trouble; I was a bit preoccupied. Ruth, this is my friend Andy Moorefield. Andy, Ruth..."

"Bannion," Ruth supplied, visibly relaxing. "And my uncle, Seth Bannion."

Andy discouraged handshakes by holding out his grimy palms and grinning.

"Ms. Dunne." Seth's tone was so bland, Lindsay thought perhaps he hadn't recognized her after all. A glimpse of his face, however, scotched the theory. Recognition was mixed with mockery. Still, the handshake was unquestionably polite, his fingers making firm but brief contact with hers. Two can play at this game, she decided.

30

"Mr. Bannion." Her tone was politely distant. "I appreciate your coming with Ruth this morning."

"My pleasure," he returned. Lindsay eyed him suspiciously.

"Let's go inside," she said directly to Ruth. Moving toward the building, she waved a quick farewell in Andy's direction, then dipped into her jacket pocket for the keys.

"It's nice of you to see me early this way, Ms. Dunne," Ruth began. Her voice was much as it had been the night before: low with a faint tremor that betrayed nerves barely under control. Lindsay noted that she clung to her uncle's arm. She smiled, touching the girl's shoulder.

"It helps me to see students individually the first time." She felt the slight resistance and casually removed her hand. "Tell me," she went on as she unlocked the studio door, "whom did you study under?"

"I've had several teachers." As she answered, Ruth stepped inside. "My father was a journalist. We were always traveling."

"I see." Lindsay glanced up at Seth, but his expression remained neutral. "If you'll just make yourself comfortable, Mr. Bannion," she said, matching his seamless politeness, "Ruth and I will work at the barre for a few moments."

Seth merely gave Lindsay a nod, but she noticed that he lightly touched Ruth's hand before he moved to a seat.

"The classes are on the small side," she began as she slipped out of her jacket. "In a town this size, I suppose we have a fairly good number of students, but we're not turning them away in droves." She smiled at Ruth, then drew white leg-warmers over her dark green tights. She wore a chiffon overskirt in a shade of sea green. Lindsay realized abruptly that the color was identical to Seth's eyes. She scowled as she reached for her ballet shoes.

"But you like to teach, don't you?" Ruth stood a few feet from her.

31

Lindsay looked up to see her, slim and uncertain in a rose pink leotard that enhanced her dark coloring. Lindsay cleared her expression before she rose.

"Yes, I do. Barre exercises first," she added, gesturing to Ruth as she herself moved to the mirrored wall. Placing her hand on the barre, she indicated for Ruth to stand in front of her. "First position."

Both figures in the mirror moved simultaneously. Both women were poised together, of nearly identical height and build. One was all light, the other stood as a dark shadow, waiting.

"*Grand plié.*"

With seemingly no effort, they dipped into deep knee bends. Lindsay watched Ruth's back, her legs, her feet for posture, positioning, style.

Slowly she began to take Ruth through the five positions, working her thoroughly. The *pliés* and *battements* were well-executed, she observed. Lindsay could see by the gesture of an arm, the movement of a leg, the love Ruth had for the dance. She remembered herself a decade before, achingly young, full of dreams and aspirations.

She smiled, recognizing a great deal of herself in Ruth. It was easy to empathize with the girl and in their joint motions to forget everything else. As her body stretched, her mind moved in close harmony.

"Toe shoes," she said abruptly, then walked away to change the CD. As she did, her eyes passed over Seth. He was watching her, and she thought there might have been something soothing in his look had it not been so uncompromisingly direct. Still, she met his eyes levelly as she slipped Tchaikovsky into the player. "We'll be about a half-hour yet, Mr. Bannion. Shall I make you some coffee?"

He didn't answer with the immediacy she expected from a casual question. The ten seconds of silence left Lindsay oddly breathless. "No," he paused, and she felt her skin grow warm. "Thank you."

When she turned away, the muscles that had been loosened at the barre were taut again. She swore under her breath but wasn't certain if she cursed Seth or herself. After gesturing for Ruth to stand in the center of the room, Lindsay walked back to the barre. She would start *adagio,* slow, sustained steps, looking for balance and style and presence. Too often in her students she found a desire only for the flash: dizzying *pirouettes, fouettés, jetés.* The beauty of a long, slow move was forgotten.

"Ready?"

"Yes, Ms. Dunne."

There was nothing shy about the girl now, Lindsay thought. She caught the light in Ruth's eyes.

"Fourth position, *pirouette,* fifth." The execution was clean, the line excellent. "Fourth position, *pirouette, attitude.*" Pleased, Lindsay began to take a slow circle around Ruth. "*Arabesque.* Again. *Attitude,* hold. *Plié.*"

Lindsay could see that Ruth had talent, and more important, she had endurance and drive. She was further gifted with the build and face of a classical dancer. Her every move was an expression of her love for the art, and Lindsay responded to her involvement. In part, Lindsay felt pain for the sacrifices and self-denial that lay ahead for Ruth, but her joy overpowered it. Here was a dancer who would make it. Excitement began to course through Lindsay's body. *And I'm going to help her,* she thought. There's still quite a bit she needs to learn. She doesn't yet know how to use her arms and hands. She has to learn to express more emotion through her face and body. But she's good—very, very good....

Nearly forty-five minutes had passed. "Relax," Lindsay said simply, then walked over to switch off the CD player. "Your several teachers appear to have done a good job." Turning back, she saw the anxiety had returned to Ruth's eyes. Instinctively, she moved to her, placing

33

her hands on her shoulders. The withdrawal was unspoken, but feeling it, Lindsay removed her hands. "I don't have to tell you that you've a great deal of talent. You're not a fool."

She watched her words sink in. The tension seemed to dissolve from Ruth's body. "It means everything to have you say it."

Surprise lifted Lindsay's brows. "Why?"

"Because you're the most wonderful dancer I've ever seen. And I know if you hadn't given it up, you'd be the most famous ballerina in the country. I've read things, too, that said you were the most promising American dancer in a decade. Davidov chose you for his partner, and he said you were the finest Juliet he ever danced with, and..." She stopped abruptly, ending the uncharacteristically long speech. Color deepened her cheeks.

Though sincerely touched, Lindsay spoke lightly to ease the embarrassment. "I'm very flattered. I don't hear nearly enough of that sort of thing around here." She paused, resisting the instinctive move to touch the girl's shoulder again. "The other girls will tell you I can be a very difficult teacher, very demanding and strict with my advanced students. You'll work hard."

"I won't mind." The gleam of anticipation had returned.

"Tell me, Ruth, what do you want?"

"To dance. To be famous," she answered immediately. "Like you."

Lindsay gave a quick laugh and shook her head. "I only wanted to dance," she told her. For a moment, the amusement flickered out. "My mother wanted me to be famous. Go, change your shoes," she said briskly. "I want to talk to your uncle now. Advanced class on Saturday is at one, *pointe* class at two-thirty. I'm a demon on punctuality." Turning, she focused on Seth. "Mr. Bannion...shall we use my office?"

Without waiting for an answer, Lindsay walked to the adjoining room.

Chapter 4

Because she wanted to establish her authority from the outset, Lindsay moved behind her desk. She felt neat and competent, light-years away from the first time she had met Seth. With a gesture for him to do likewise, she sat. Ignoring the instruction, Seth stood, scanning the photographs on her wall. She saw that he had focused on one of herself and Nick Davidov in the final act of *Romeo and Juliet*.

"I managed to get my hands on a poster from this ballet and sent it to Ruth some years back. She has it in her room still." He turned back but didn't move to her. "She admires you tremendously." Though his tone was even, Lindsay understood he felt the admiration implied responsibility. She frowned, not because she was loath to take it, but because he gave it to her.

"As Ruth's guardian," she began, circling around his statement, "I feel you should know precisely what it is she'll be doing here, what's expected of her, when the classes are set and so forth."

"I believe you're the expert in this field, Ms. Dunne." Seth's voice was quiet, but Lindsay wasn't certain his mind was on his words. Again his eyes roamed her face inch by inch. It was odd, she thought, that his manner and tone could be so formal while his gaze was so personal. She shifted, suddenly uncomfortable.

"As her guardian…"

"As her guardian," Seth interrupted, "I'm aware that studying ballet is as necessary to Ruth as breathing." He came closer now, so that she had to tilt her head back to keep her eyes on his. "I'm also aware that I have to trust you…to an extent."

Lindsay lifted a brow curiously. "To what extent is that?"

"I'll know better in a couple of weeks. I like my information to be more complete before I make a decision." The eyes that were fixed on her face narrowed ever so slightly. "I don't know you yet."

She nodded, miffed without knowing precisely why. "Nor I you."

"True." He took the statement without a change of expression. "I suppose that's a problem that will solve itself in time. It's difficult for me to believe that the Lindsay Dunne I saw dance Giselle is clumsy enough to fall into puddles."

She sucked in her breath, staring at him in outraged amazement. "You nearly ran me down!" All the restraint she had practiced that morning vanished. "Anyone who comes barreling down a residential street in the rain that way should be arrested."

"Fifteen miles an hour isn't considered barreling," he countered mildly. "If I'd been doing the speed limit, I *would* have run you down. You weren't looking where you were going."

"Most people take a little care to learn the streets when they move into a new neighborhood," Lindsay retorted.

"Most people don't go for walks in rain storms," he returned. "I've an appointment shortly," he continued before she could answer. "Shall I write you a check for Ruth's tuition?"

"I'll send you a bill," she told him icily, walking past him to open the door.

Seth followed her, then pausing, crowded her into the jamb as he turned to face her again. Their bodies brushed in brief, potent contact. Every coherent thought veered out of Lindsay's brain. Tilting her head, she stared up at him, surprised and questioning, while her body reacted with instinctual knowledge.

For a moment he stayed, his eyes again making their slow, intruding study before he turned and walked to Ruth.

Off and on during the day, Lindsay's thoughts returned to Seth Bannion. What sort of man was he? On the surface he appeared to be conventional enough. But there was something more beneath. It wasn't just the glimpse of his temper she had witnessed in their first meeting. She had seen something in his eyes, felt something in the touch of his body. It was an energy that went further than the physical. She knew that volcanoes were usually calm and well-mannered on the surface but that there was always something hot and dangerous underneath.

It's nothing to me, she reminded herself, but her thoughts drifted back to him more often than she liked. He interested her. And so did his niece.

Lindsay watched Ruth during her first two classes, looking for more than technique and movement. She wanted to discover attitude and personality. Outgoing herself, Lindsay found it difficult to understand the guards the girl had built. She made no move to reach out to any of her fellow students nor to accept any overtures made to her. She was not unfriendly nor impolite, simply distant. It would be her fate, Lindsay knew, to be labeled a snob. But it isn't snobbery, Lindsay mused as she took her class through *glissades*. It's overwhelming insecurity. Lindsay recalled the instant withdrawal when she had laid her hands on Ruth's shoulders. She remembered how Ruth had been clinging to Seth before the morning session. He's her anchor at the moment; I wonder if he knows it, she mused. How much does he know about her doubts and her fears and the reason for them? How much does he care?

Lindsay demonstrated a move, her body lifting effortlessly to *pointe,* her arms rising slowly. His doubts about her training seemed to Lindsay inconsistent with his patience in sitting through the morning session.

It annoyed her that once again he had insinuated himself into her thoughts. Thrusting him out, Lindsay concentrated fully on the last of her classes. But even as her final student dashed through the front door, leaving her alone, her defenses slipped. She remembered the exploring way he had looked at her and the quiet, even texture of his voice.

Trouble, she thought as she stacked CDs. *Complications.* I'm beginning to enjoy life without complications. She glanced around with a satisfied smile.

My studio, she thought chauvinistically. I'm making something out of it. It might be small and filled with girls who won't dance to anything but top-forty rock after they hit sixteen, but it's mine. I'm making a living doing something I enjoy. What else could anyone want? Irresistibly, her eyes were drawn down to the CD she still held in her hand. Without hesitation, she inserted it into the player.

She loved her students, and she loved teaching them, but she also loved the empty studio. She had found satisfaction in the past three years of instructing, but there was something private—something nourishing—in dancing for the sheer sake of it. It was something her mother had never understood. To Mae, dancing was a commitment, and obsession. To Lindsay, it was a joy, a lover.

Ruth had brought back memories of Dulcinea. It had always been a favored role of Lindsay's because of its enthusiasm and power. Now, as the music poured into the room, she remembered vividly the flow of movement and the strength.

The music was fast and richly Spanish, and she responded to it with verve. Her body came to life with the need to dance. The challenge of the story came back to her to be expressed with sharp arm movements and *soubresauts*. There was energy and youth in the short, quick steps.

As she danced, the mirror reflected the gently flowing chiffon, but in Lindsay's mind, she wore the stiff tutu in black lace and red satin. There was a full-blossomed rose behind her ear and a Spanish comb in her hair. She was Dulcinea, all spirit, all challenge, with the energy to dance endlessly. As the music built toward the finish, Lindsay began her *fouettés*. Around and around with speed and style she twirled herself. It seemed she could go on forever, like the ballerina on a music box, effortlessly spinning to the tune. And as the toy stopped with the music, so did she. She threw a hand over her head and the other to her waist, styling for the sassy ending.

"Bravo."

With both hands clasped to her speeding heart, she whirled. There, straddling one of her small, wooden chairs, was Seth Bannion. She was breathing heavily, both from the exertion of the dance and from the shock of discovering she had not been alone. Her eyes were huge, still dark with excitement, her skin wildly flushed.

The dance had been for herself alone, but she felt no infringement on her privacy. There was no resentment that he had shared it with her. Even her initial surprise was fading to be replaced by an inner knowledge that he would understand what she had been doing and why. She didn't question the feeling, but stood, waiting as he rose and moved to her.

He kept his eyes on hers, and something more than breathlessness began to flutter inside her breast. The look was long and personal. Her blood, already warmed from the dance, heated further. She could feel it tingle under the surface of her skin. There was a feathery dryness in her throat. She lifted one of the hands she still held against her breast and pressed it to her lips.

"Magnificent," he murmured with his eyes still locked on hers. He took the hand she had pressed to her lips and brought it to his own. Her pulse was still racing at her wrist, and his thumb grazed it lightly. "You make it seem so effortless," he commented. "I hardly expect you to be out of breath."

The smile he gave her was as potent as it was unexpected. "I feel I should thank you, even though the dance wasn't for me."

"I didn't...I wasn't expecting anyone." Her voice was as jumpy as her nerves, and Lindsay sought to discipline them both. She began to remove her hand from his and was surprised when Seth resisted, holding her fingers an extra moment before releasing them.

"No, I could see you weren't." He took yet another careful scan of her face. "I'd apologize for intruding, but I'm not in the least bit sorry to have been your audience." He possessed considerably more charm than Lindsay had given him credit for. It made it difficult to separate her response to the dance from her response to him. She thought the slight wings at the tips of his brows were fascinating. Only when the left one tilted up did she realize she'd been staring and that he was amused by it. Annoyed with her own lack of sophistication, she turned to the CD player.

"I don't mind," she told him carelessly. "I always worked better with an audience. Was there something you wanted to talk to me about?"

"My knowledge of ballet is limited. What was the dance from?"

"Don Quixote." Lindsay slipped the CD back into its case. "Ruth reminded me of it last night." She faced Seth again with the CD held between them. "She intends to dance Dulcinea one day."

"And will she?" Seth took the CD from her hands, setting it aside as if impatient with the barrier.

"I think so. She has exceptional talent." Lindsay gave him a direct look. "Why did you come back here?"

He smiled again, a slow, somehow dashing smile she knew women found difficult to resist. "To see you," he said and continued to smile as surprise reflected clearly on her face. "And to talk about Ruth. It simply wasn't possible this morning."

"I see." Lindsay nodded, prepared to become the instructor again. "There is quite a bit we need to discuss. I'm afraid I thought you weren't terribly interested this morning."

"I'm very interested." His eyes were on hers again. "Have dinner with me."

It took Lindsay a moment to react, as her mind had jumped forward to plans for Ruth. "Dinner?" She gave him an ingenuous stare as she tried to decide how she felt about the idea of being with him. "I don't know if I want to do that."

His brows lifted at her bluntness, but he nodded. "Then you apparently haven't any great objection. I'll pick you up at seven." Before she could comment, Seth walked back to the door. "I already know the address."

When she had bought it, Lindsay had thought the pelican gray dress would be clean and sophisticated. It was made of thin, soft wool and was closely tailored with a mandarin collar. Critically studying herself in it, she was pleased. This was a far different image than the dripping, babbling mess who had sat in a roadside puddle, and more

41

different, still, from the dreamy, absorbed dancer. The woman who stared back at Lindsay from the glass was a confident, mature woman. She felt as comfortable with this image as she felt with all her other roles. She decided that this aspect of Lindsay Dunne would deal most successfully with Seth Bannion. Lindsay brushed her long mane of hair over one shoulder and braided it loosely as she thought of him.

He intrigued her, perhaps because she hadn't been able to pigeon-hole him, as she often did with the people she met. She sensed he was complex, and complexities always had interested her. Or perhaps, she thought, fastening thick, silver hoops to her ears, it was just because he had bought the Cliff House.

Moving to the closet, Lindsay took out his jacket and folded it. It occurred to her suddenly that it had been some time since her last real date. There had been movies and quick dinners with Andy, but thinking back on them, she decided those times hardly counted as dates. Andy's like my brother, she mused, unconsciously toying with the collar of Seth's jacket. His scent still clung to it, faint but unmis-takably male.

How long has it been since I went out with a man? she wondered. Three months? Four? Six, she decided with a sigh. And in the past three years, no more than a handful of times. Before that? Lindsay laughed and shook her head. Before that, a date had been the next performance scheduled.

Did she regret it? For a moment she studied herself seriously in the glass. There was a young woman there whose fragile looks were deceptive, whose mouth was generous. No, she'd never regretted it. How could she? She had what she wanted, and whatever she had lost was balanced on the other end of the scale. Glancing up, she saw the reflection of her toe shoes in the mirror as they hung over her bed.

Thoughtfully, she stroked the collar of Seth's jacket again before gathering it up with her purse.

Her heels clicked lightly on the stair treads as she came down to the main floor. A quick glance at her watch assured her that she had a few minutes to spare. Setting down the jacket and her purse, Lindsay walked back toward her mother's rooms.

Since Mae's return from the hospital, she had been confined to the first floor of the house. Initially, the stairs had been too much for her to manage, and afterward, the habit of avoiding them had set in. The arrangement afforded both women privacy. Two rooms off the kitchen had been converted to serve as Mae's bedroom and sitting room. For the first year, Lindsay had slept on the sofa in the living room to be within calling distance. Even now she slept lightly, ever alert for any disturbance in the night.

She paused at her mother's rooms, hearing the low drone of the television. After knocking softly, she opened the door.

"Mother, I..."

She stopped when she saw Mae sitting in the recliner. Her legs were propped up as she faced the television, but her attention was focused on the book in her lap. Lindsay knew the book well. It was long and wide and leather-bound to endure wear. Nearly half of its oversized pages were crammed with clippings and photos. There were professional critiques, gossip column tidbits and interviews, all expounding on Lindsay Dunne's dancing career. There was the earliest story from the *Cliffside Daily* to her final review in the *New York Times*. Her professional life—and a good portion of her personal one as well—were bound in that book.

As always, when she saw her mother poring over the scrapbook, Lindsay was struck by waves of guilt and helplessness. She felt her frustration rise as she stepped into the room.

"Mother."

This time Mae glanced up. Her eyes were lit with excitement, her cheeks flushed with it. "'A lyrical dancer,'" she quoted without looking back at the clipping, "'with the beauty and grace of a fairy tale. Breathtaking.' Clifford James," Mae continued, watching Lindsay as she crossed the room. "One of the toughest dance critics in the business. You were only nineteen."

"I was overwhelmed by that review," Lindsay remembered, smiling as she laid her hand on her mother's shoulder. "I don't think my feet touched ground for a week."

"He'd say the same thing if you went back today."

Lindsay shifted her attention from the clipping and met her mother's eyes. A thin thread of tension made its way up her neck. "Today I'm twenty-five," she reminded her gently.

"He would," Mae insisted. "We both know it. You…"

"Mother." Sharply, Lindsay cut her off, then, appalled by her own tone, crouched down beside the chair. "I'm sorry, I don't want to talk about this now. Please." She lifted their joined hands to her cheek, and sighing, wished there could be more between them than the dance. "I've only another minute or two."

Mae studied her daughter's dark, expressive eyes and saw the plea. She shifted restlessly in her chair. "Carol didn't say anything about your going out tonight."

Reminded that Andy's mother had spent part of the day with her mother, Lindsay rose and began a cautious explanation. "I'm not going out with Andy." She straightened the line of her dress.

"No?" Mae frowned. "Who, then?"

"The uncle of a new student of mine." Lindsay brought her head up to meet Mae's eyes. "She has potential, a truly natural talent. I'd like you to see her."

"What about him?" Mae brushed off the thought of Lindsay's student and stared down at the open scrapbook.

"I don't know him very well, of course. He's bought the Cliff House."

"Oh?" Mae's attention returned. She was aware of Lindsay's fascination with the house.

"Yes, they've just recently moved in. It seems Ruth was orphaned a few months ago." She paused, remembering the sadness lurking in the girl's eyes. "She interests me very much. I want to speak to her uncle about her."

"So you're having dinner."

"That's right." Annoyed at having to justify a simple date, Lindsay moved to the door. "I don't suppose I'll be very late. Would you like anything before I go?"

"I'm not a cripple."

Lindsay's eyes flew to her mother's. Mae's mouth was set, her fingers gripped tight on the edges of the book. "I know."

Then there was a silence between them that Lindsay felt unable to break. Why is it, she wondered, that the longer I live with her, the wider the gap? The doorbell sounded, overloud in the quiet. Studying her daughter, Mae recognized the indecision. She broke the contact by looking back at the pages in her lap.

"Good night, Lindsay."

She tasted failure as she turned to the door. "Good night."

Briskly, Lindsay walked down the hall, struggling out of the mood. There was nothing I could have done differently, she told herself. Nothing I could have altered. Suddenly she wanted escape, she wanted to open the front door, to step outside and to keep going until she was somewhere else. Anywhere else. Someplace where she could take her time discovering what it was she really wanted of herself. Lindsay pulled open the door with a hint of desperation.

"Hi." She greeted Seth with a smile as she stepped back to let him in. The dark suit was perfect for his lean, elegant build. Still, there was something slightly sinful about his face. It was dark and narrow and knowing. Lindsay found she liked the contrast. "I suppose I need a coat; it's turned cold." She walked to the hall closet to take out a coat of dark leather. Seth took it from her.

Wordlessly, she allowed him to slip the coat over her while she wondered about basic chemistry. It was odd, she thought, that one person should have such a strong physical reaction to another. Wasn't it strange that nearness or a touch or just a look could increase the heartbeat or raise the blood pressure? Nothing else was required— no personal knowledge, no amiability—just that chance mixture of chemicals. Lindsay didn't resist when Seth turned her to face him. They stood very close, eyes holding, as he brought his hand from her shoulder to adjust the collar of her coat.

"Do you think it's strange," she asked thoughtfully, "that I should be so strongly attracted to you when I thought you were quite horrible the first time I met you, and I'm still not completely sure you're not?"

His grin was different from his smile, she noted. The smile was slow, while the grin was a quick flash. All of his features responded at once. "Are your sentences always so frank and so convoluted?"

"Probably." Lindsay turned away, pleased to have seen the grin. "I'm not very good at dissimulating, and I suppose I talk as I think. Here's your jacket." She handed it to him, dry and neatly folded. Her smile came easily. "I certainly didn't expect to return it to you under these circumstances."

Seth took it, glancing at it briefly before bringing his eyes back to hers. "Did you have other circumstances in mind?"

"Several," Lindsay answered immediately as she picked up her purse. "And you were extremely uncomfortable in all of them. In one, you were serving a ten-year stretch for insulting dancers on rainy afternoons. Are we ready?" she asked, holding out her hand to him in a habitual gesture. His hesitation was almost too brief to measure before he accepted it. Their fingers interlocked.

"You're not what I expected," Seth told her as they stepped out into the chill of the night.

"No?" Lindsay took a deep breath, lifting her face to try to take in all the stars at once. "What did you expect?"

They walked to the car in silence, and Lindsay could smell the spicy aroma of mums and rotting leaves. When they were in the car, Seth turned to her to give her another of the long, probing looks she had come to expect of him.

"The image you were portraying this morning was more in line with what I expected," he said at length. "Very professional, very cool and detached."

"I had fully intended to continue along those lines this evening," Lindsay informed him. "Then I forgot."

"Will you tell me why you looked ready to run for your life when you answered the door?"

She lifted a brow. "You're very perceptive."

With a sigh, Lindsay sat back against the seat. "It has to do with my mother and a constant feeling of inadequacy." She twisted her head until her eyes met his. "Perhaps one day I'll tell you about it," she murmured, not pausing to ponder why she felt she could. "But not tonight. I don't want to think about it anymore tonight."

"All right." Seth started the car. "Then perhaps you'll let a new resident in on who's who in Cliffside."

Lindsay relaxed, grateful. "How far away is the restaurant?"

"About twenty minutes," he told her.

"That should about do it," she decided, and she began to fill him in.

47

Chapter 5

Lindsay felt comfortable with Seth. She told him amusing stories because she liked the sound of his laughter. Her own mood of panic and desperation was gone. As they drove, she decided she wanted to know him better. She was intrigued and attracted, and if something volcanic erupted, she'd risk it. Natural disasters were rarely dull.

Lindsay knew the restaurant. She had been there once or twice before when a date had wanted to impress her. She knew that Seth Bannion wouldn't feel the need to impress anyone. This was simply the sort of restaurant he could choose: quiet, elegant, with superior food and service.

"My father brought me here once," Lindsay remembered as she stepped from the car. "On my sixteenth birthday." She waited for Seth to join her, then offered her hand. "I hadn't been allowed to date until then, so he took me out on my birthday. He said he wanted to be my first date." She smiled, warmed by the memory. "He was always doing things like that...small, incredible things." Turning, she found Seth watching her. Moonlight showered over both of them. "I'm glad I came. I'm glad it was with you."

He gave her a curious look, then trailed a finger down her braid. "So am I."

Together they walked up the steps that led to the front door.

Inside, Lindsay was attracted to the long, wide window that revealed an expanse of the Long Island Sound. Sitting in the warm, candlelit restaurant, she could all but hear the waves beat against the rocks below. She could almost feel the cold and the spray.

"This is a wonderful place," she enthused as they settled at their table. "So elegant, so subdued, yet open to all that power." There was a smile on her lips as she turned back to Seth. "I like contrasts, don't you?" The candlelight caught the dull gleam of silver at her ears. "How dull life would be if everything fit into a slot."

"I've been wondering," Seth countered as his eyes flickered from the thick hoops to the delicate planes of her face, "exactly where you fit in."

After a quick shake of her head, Lindsay looked back out the window. "I often wonder that myself. You know yourself well, I think. It shows."

"Would you like something to drink?"

Lindsay turned her head at Seth's question and saw a waiter hovering at his elbow. "Yes." She smiled at him before she gave her attention back to Seth. "Some white wine would be nice, I think. Something cold and dry."

His eyes remained on hers while he ordered. There's something quietly tenacious in the way he looks at me, Lindsay decided, like a man who's finished one page of a book and intends to go on reading until the end. When they were alone, the silence held. Something fluttered up her spine, and she drew in a long breath. It was time to establish priorities.

"We need to talk about Ruth."

"Yes."

"Seth." Nonplussed that his look didn't waver, Lindsay added authority to her voice. "You have to stop looking at me that way."

"I don't think so," he disagreed mildly.

Her brow arched at his reply, but a hint of amusement touched her mouth. "And I thought you were so scrupulously polite."

"I'm adaptable," he told her. He was relaxed in his chair, one arm resting over the back as he studied her. "You're beautiful. I enjoy looking at beauty."

"Thank you." Lindsay decided she would grow used to his direct gaze before the evening was over. "Seth," she leaned forward, pushed by her own thoughts, "this morning, when I watched Ruth, I knew she had talent. This afternoon in class I was even more impressed."

"It was very important to her to study with you."

"But it shouldn't be." Lindsay continued quickly as she again observed the slight narrowing of his eyes. "I'm not capable of giving her everything she needs. My school's so limited in what it can offer, especially to a girl like Ruth. She should be in New York, in a school where her training could be more centered, more intense."

Seth waited while the waiter opened and poured their wine. He lifted his glass, studying the contents carefully before speaking. "Aren't you capable of instructing Ruth?"

Lindsay's brows shot up at the tone of the question. When she answered, her voice was no longer warm. "I'm a capable instructor. Ruth simply needs discipline and advantages available elsewhere."

"You're easily annoyed," Seth commented, then sipped his wine.

"Am I?" Lindsay sipped hers as well, trying to remain as pragmatic as he. "Perhaps I'm temperamental," she offered and felt satisfied with the cool tone. "You've probably heard dancers are high-strung."

50

Seth shifted his shoulders. "Ruth plans to take more than fifteen hours of training a week with you. Isn't that adequate?"

"No." Lindsay set down her glass and again leaned close. If he asked questions, she concluded, he couldn't be totally unreasonable. "She should be taking classes every day, more specialized classes than I could possibly offer because I simply don't have any other students with her abilities. Even if I could instruct her one on one, it wouldn't be enough. She needs partnering classes. I have four male students, all of whom come in once a week to polish their football moves. They won't even participate in the recitals."

A sound of frustration escaped. Her voice had become low and intense in her need to make him understand. "Cliffside isn't the cultural center of the east coast. It's a small Yankee town." There was an inherent, unrehearsed beauty in the way her hands gestured to accent her words. Music was in the movement, silent and sweet. "People here are basic, they're not dreamers. Dancing has no practical purpose. It can be a hobby, it can be an enjoyment, but here it isn't thought of as a career. It's not thought of as a life."

"Yet you grew up here," Seth pointed out, then added more wine to the glasses. It shimmered gold in the candlelight. "You made it a career."

"That's true." Lindsay ran a fingertip around the rim of her glass. She hesitated, wanting to choose her words carefully. "My mother was a professional dancer, and she was very...strict about my training. I went to a school about seventy miles from here. We spent a great deal of time in the car coming and going." Again she looked up at Seth, but the smile was beginning to play around her mouth. "My teacher was a marvel, a wonderful woman, half French, half Russian. She's almost seventy now and not taking students or I'd plead with you to send Ruth to her."

Seth's tone was as calm and undisturbed as it had been at the start of the conversation. "Ruth wants to study with you."

Lindsay wanted to scream with frustration. She took a sip of wine until the feeling passed. "I was seventeen, Ruth's age, when I went to New York. And I'd already had eight years of intense study in a larger school. At eighteen I started with the company. The competition for a place is brutal, and training is..." Lindsay paused, then laughed and shook her head. "It's indescribable. Ruth needs it, she deserves it. As soon as possible if she wants to be a serious dancer. Her talent demands it."

Seth took his time in answering. "Ruth is little more than a child who's just been through a series of unhappy events." He signaled the waiter for menus. "New York will still be there in three or four years."

"Three or four years!" Lindsay set the menu down without glancing at it. She stared at Seth, incredulous. "She'll be twenty."

"An advanced age," he returned dryly.

"It is for a dancer," Lindsay retorted. "It's rare for one of us to dance much past thirty. Oh, the men steal a few extra years with character parts, or now and again there's someone spectacular like Fonteyn. Those are the exceptions, not the rules."

"Is that why you don't go back?" Lindsay's thoughts stumbled to a halt at the question. "Do you feel your career is over at twenty-five?"

She lifted her glass, then set it down again. "We're discussing Ruth," she reminded him, "not me."

"Mysteries are intriguing, Lindsay." Seth picked up her hand, turning it over to study her palm before he brought his eyes back to hers. "And a beautiful woman with secrets is irresistible. Have you ever considered that some hands were made for kissing? This is one of them." He took her palm to his lips.

Lindsay's muscles seemed to go fluid at the contact. She studied him, frankly fascinated with the sensations. She wondered what it would feel like to have his lips pressed to hers, firmly, warmly. She liked the shape of his mouth and the slow, considering way it smiled. Abruptly, she brought herself out of the dream. *Priorities,* she remembered.

"About Ruth," she began. Though she tried to pull her hand away, Seth kept it in his.

"Ruth's parents were killed in a train accident barely six months ago. It was in Italy." There was no increased pressure on her fingers, but his voice had tightened. His eyes had hardened. Lindsay was reminded of how he had looked when he had loomed over her in the rain. "Ruth was unusually close to them, perhaps because they traveled so much. It was difficult for her to form other attachments. You might be able to imagine what it was like for a sixteen-year-old girl to find herself suddenly orphaned in a foreign country, in a town they'd been in for only two weeks."

Lindsay's eyes filled with painful sympathy, but he continued before she could speak. "She knew virtually no one, and as I was on a site in South Africa, it took days to contact me. She was on her own for nearly a week before I could get to her. My brother and his wife were already buried when I got there."

"Seth, I'm sorry. I'm so terribly sorry." The need to comfort was instinctive. Lindsay's fingers tightened on his as her other hand reached up to cover their joined ones. Something flickered in his eyes, but she was too overwhelmed to see it. "It must have been horrible for her, for you."

He didn't speak for a moment, but his study of her face deepened. "Yes," he said at length, "it was. I brought Ruth back to the States, but New York is very demanding, and she was very fragile."

"So you found the Cliff House," Lindsay murmured.

Seth lifted a brow at the title but didn't comment. "I wanted to

53

give her something stable for a while, though I know she's not thrilled with the notion of settling into a house in a small town. She's too much like her father. But for now, I feel it's what she needs."

"I think I can understand what you're trying to do," Lindsay said slowly. "And I respect it, but Ruth has other needs as well."

"We'll talk about them in six months."

The tone was so final and quietly authoritative that Lindsay had closed her mouth before she realized it. Annoyance flitted over her face. "You're very dictatorial, aren't you?"

"So I've been told." His mood seemed to switch as she looked on. "Hungry?" he asked and smiled with slow deliberation.

"A bit," she admitted, but she frowned as she opened the menu. "The stuffed lobster is especially good here."

As Seth ordered, Lindsay let her eyes drift back out to the Sound. Clearly, she could see Ruth alone, frightened, stunned with grief, having to deal with the loss of her parents and the dreadful details that must have followed. Too well could she recall the panic she had felt upon being notified of her own parents' accident. There was no forgetting the horror of the trip from New York back to Connecticut to find her father dead and her mother in a coma.

And I was an adult, she reminded herself, already having been on my own for over three years. I was in my hometown, surrounded by friends. More than ever, she felt the need to help Ruth.

Six months, she mused. If I can work with her individually, the time wouldn't be completely wasted. And maybe, just maybe, I can convince Seth sooner. He's got to understand how important this is for her. Losing my temper isn't going to get me anywhere with a man like this, she acknowledged, so I'll have to find some other way.

On a site in South Africa, Lindsay reflected, going back over their conversation. Now what would he have been doing in South Africa?

Even before she could mull over the possibilities, a jingle of memory sounded in her brain.

"Bannion," she said aloud and sent his eyebrow up in question. "S. N. Bannion, the architect. It just came to me."

"Did it?" He seemed mildly surprised, then broke a breadstick in half. He offered her a share. "I'm surprised you've had time to delve into architecture."

"I'd have to have been living in a cave for the past ten years not to know the name. What was it in... *Newsview?* Yes, *Newsview,* about a year ago. There was a profile of you with pictures of some of your more prestigious buildings. The Trade Center in Zurich, the MacAfee Building in San Diego."

"Your memory's excellent," Seth commented. The candlelight marbled over her skin. She looked as fragile as porcelain with eyes dark and vivid. They seemed to smile at him.

"Flawless," Lindsay agreed. "I also recall reading several tidbits about you and a large portion of the female population. I distinctly remember a department store heiress, an Australian tennis pro and a Spanish opera star. Weren't you engaged to Billie Marshall, the newscaster, a few months ago?"

Seth twirled the stem of his glass between his fingers. "I've never been engaged," he answered simply. "It tends to lead to marriage."

"I see." Absently, she chewed on the breadstick. "And that isn't one of your goals?"

"Is it one of yours?" he countered.

Lindsay paused, frowning. She took his parry quite seriously. "I don't know," she murmured. "I suppose I've never thought of it in precisely that way. Actually, I haven't had a great deal of time to think of it at all. Should it be a goal?" she thought aloud. "Or more of a surprise, an adventure?"

"So speaks the romantic," Seth observed.

"Yes, I am," Lindsay agreed without embarrassment. "But then, so are you or you'd never have bought the Cliff House."

"My choice of real estate makes me a romantic?"

Lindsay leaned back, still nibbling on the breadstick. "It's much more than a piece of real estate, and I've no doubt you felt that, too. You could have bought a dozen houses, all more conveniently located and in less need of repair."

"Why didn't I?" Seth asked, intrigued with her theory.

Lindsay allowed him to top off her glass again but left it untouched. The effect of the wine was already swirling pleasantly in her head. "Because you recognized the charm, the uniqueness. If you were a cynic, you'd have bought one of the condos twenty miles further up the coast which claim to put you in touch with genuine New England scenery while being fifteen convenient minutes from the Yankee Trader Mall."

Seth laughed, keeping his eyes on her while their meal was served. "I take it you don't care for condos."

"I detest them," Lindsay agreed immediately. "Arbitrarily, I'm afraid, but that's strictly personal. They're perfect for a great number of people. I don't like..." She trailed off, hands gesturing as if to pluck the word from the air. "Uniformity," she decided. "That's strange, I suppose, because there's so much regimentation in my career. I see that differently. Individual expression is so vital. I'd so much rather someone say I was different than I was beautiful." She glanced down at the enormous serving of lobster. "*Innovative* is such a marvelous word," she stated. "I've heard it applied to you."

"Is that why you became a dancer?" Seth speared a delicate morsel of lobster into melted butter. "To express yourself?"

"I think it might be that because I was a dancer, I craved self-expression." Lindsay chose lemon over butter. "Actually, I don't analyze myself often, just other people. Did you know the house was haunted?"

"No." He grinned. "That wasn't brought up during settlement."

"That's because they were afraid you'd back out." Lindsay speared a piece of lobster. "It's too late now, and in any case, I think you'd enjoy having a ghost."

"Would you?"

"Oh, yes, I would. Tremendously." She popped the lobster into her mouth, leaning forward. "It's a romantic, forlorn creature who was done in by a narrow-minded husband about a century ago. She was sneaking off to see her lover and was careless, I suppose. In any case, he dropped her from the second-floor balcony onto the rocks."

"That should have discouraged her adulterous tendencies," Seth commented.

"Mmm," she agreed with a nod, hampered by a full mouth. "But she comes back now and again to walk in the garden. That's where her lover was waiting."

"You seem rather pleased about the murder and deceit."

"A hundred years can make almost anything romantic. Do you realize how many of the great ballets deal with death yet remain romantic? *Giselle* and *Romeo and Juliet* are only two."

"And you've played both leads," Seth said. "Perhaps that's why you emphathize with a star-crossed ghost."

"Oh, I was involved with your ghost before I danced either Giselle or Juliet," Lindsay sighed, watching the stars glitter over the water's surface. "That house has fascinated me for as long as I can remember. When I was a child, I swore I'd live there one day. I'd have the gardens replanted, and all the windows would glisten in the sun." She turned back to Seth. "That's why I'm glad you bought it."

"Are you?" His eyes ran the length of her slender throat to the collar of her dress. "Why?"

"Because you'll appreciate it. You'll know what to do to make it live again." His gaze paused briefly on her mouth before returning to her eyes. Lindsay felt a tingle along her skin. She straightened in her chair. "I know you've done some work already," she continued, feeling the Cliff House was a safe dinner topic. "You must have specific plans for changes."

"Would you like to see what's been done?"

"Yes," she answered immediately, unable to pretend otherwise.

"I'll pick you up tomorrow afternoon." He looked at her curiously. "Did you know you've an outrageous appetite for someone so small?"

Lindsay laughed, at ease again, and buttered a roll.

The sky was a deep, dark blue. The stars were low and bright, glimmering through a cloudy sky. Lindsay could feel the autumn wind shiver against the car as Seth drove along the coast. It added excitement to the romance of moonlight and wine.

The evening, she decided, had been much more pleasant than she had anticipated. From the first moment, she had enjoyed being with him. It surprised her that he could make her laugh. Lindsay knew there were times between dealing with her work and her mother that she became too serious, too intense. It was good to have someone to laugh with.

By unspoken agreement, they had steered away from controversial topics, keeping the conversation as light and palatable as the meal. She knew they would lock horns again over Ruth; there was no escaping it. Their desires for her were so totally diverse that no solution could be reached without a battle. Or two. But for the moment, Lindsay felt calm. Even as she wondered about the eye of the storm, she accepted it.

"I love nights like this," she said on a sigh. "Nights when the stars hang low and the wind talks in the trees. You'd hear the water from the east side of your house." She turned to him as she spoke. "Did you take the bedroom with the balcony that hangs over the Sound? The one that has an adjoining dressing room?"

Seth turned to her briefly. "You seem to know the house well."

Lindsay laughed. "You could hardly expect me to resist exploring the place when it was just sitting there waiting."

Ahead, a few twinkling lights outlined Cliffside against the darkness. "Is that the room you've taken?"

"The huge stone fireplace and lofty old ceiling would have been enough by themselves, but the balcony... Have you stood on it during a storm?" she demanded. "It must be incredible with the waves crashing and the wind and lightning so close." Her eyes were trained on him so that she saw the tilt of his smile when it began.

"You like to live dangerously."

She wondered how his hair would feel between her fingers. Her eyes widened at the route her thoughts had taken. Carefully, she laced her fingers in her lap. "I suppose," she began, going back to his comment. "Perhaps I never have, except vicariously. Cliffside isn't exactly fraught with danger."

"Tell that to your ghost."

Lindsay chuckled. "*Your* ghost," she corrected as he pulled up in front of her house. "You've absolute claim on her now." While she spoke, Lindsay stepped from the car. The wind fluttered over her face. "It's truly fall now," she mused, looking about her at the quiet house. "We'll have a bonfire in the square. Marshall Woods will bring his fiddle, and there'll be music until midnight." She smiled. "It's a

59

big event in town. I suppose it must seem very tame to someone who's traveled as much as you have."

"I grew up in a dot on the map in Iowa," he told her as they passed through the gate.

"Did you really?" Lindsay mulled over the information. "Somehow I pictured you growing up in a city, very urbane, very sophisticated. Why didn't you go back?" She stood on the first step of the porch and turned to him again.

"Too many memories."

With the height of the step and her evening shoes, Lindsay stood nearly level with him. There was a jolt of surprise in finding her eyes and mouth lined up with his. In his irises were tiny amber flecks. Without thinking, she counted them.

"There are thirteen," she murmured. "Six in one and seven in the other. I wonder if it's bad luck."

"If what's bad luck?" Her eyes were direct on his, but he could see her mind drift off, then snap back at his question.

"Oh, nothing." Lindsay brushed off the question, embarrassed by her lapse. "I have a tendency to daydream." Amusement moved over Seth's face. "Why are you smiling?"

"I was thinking back on the last time I walked my girl to her door with the front porch light shining behind her and her mother inside. I think I was eighteen."

Lindsay's eyes brightened with mischief. "It's a comfort to know you were eighteen once. Did you kiss her good-night?"

"Naturally. While her mother peeked through the living room drapes."

Slowly, Lindsay twisted her head and studied the dark, empty windows. With an arching brow, she turned back. "Mine's probably gone to bed by now," she decided. Laying her hands on

60

his shoulders, Lindsay leaned forward to touch her lips lightly, quickly, to his.

In an instant of contact, everything changed. The bare brushing of lips was cataclysmic. Its effect rocketed through her with such velocity that she gasped. Carefully she drew away, still keeping her hands on his shoulders as they studied each other.

Her heart was knocking against her ribs as it had when she had stood in the wings before a difficult *pas de deux*. Anticipation soared through her. But this duet was unrehearsed and older than time. She dropped her eyes to his mouth and felt a hunger that was essentially physical.

They came together slowly, as if time would stop for them. There was a certainty as they slipped into each other's arms, as of old lovers reacquainting rather than meeting for the first time. Their lips touched and parted, touched and parted, as they experimented with angles. His hands slid inside her coat, hers inside his jacket. Warmth grew as the wind swirled a few autumn leaves around them.

Seth caught her bottom lip between his teeth to halt her roaming mouth. The tiny nick of pain shot trembles of desire through her. Passion flared. The slow, experimental kisses became one desperate demand. Her tongue moved with his. The hunger intensified, promising only to increase with each taste. Lindsay curved her arms up his back until she gripped his shoulders. She pressed hard against him as he took his mouth from hers to move it to the slender arch of her throat. His hair feathered against her cheek. It was soft and cool, unlike the heat of his mouth, and it seemed to draw her fingers into it.

She felt him tug the zipper of her dress down until his hands touched the naked skin of her back. They roamed, trailing down to her waist and up to the nape of her neck, flashing flames along the journey. The longing for him swelled so urgently that Lindsay trembled with it before his mouth at last returned to hers.

Her emotions began to swirl, rising to compete with the physical need. The onslaught made her dizzy, the intensity frightening her. She was discovering frailties she had not known she possessed. Struggling back to the surface, Lindsay brought her hands to his chest to push herself away. Seth freed her lips, though he kept her close in his arms.

"No, I..." Lindsay closed her eyes briefly, drawing back the strength she had always taken for granted. "It was a lovely evening, Seth. I appreciate it."

He watched her in silence a moment. "Don't you think that little speech is a bit out of place now?" Barely moving, he rubbed her lips with his.

"Yes, yes, you're right, but..." Lindsay turned her head and breathed deep of the cool, evening air. "I have to go in. I'm out of practice."

Seth took her chin in his hand, turning her face back to his. "Practice?"

Lindsay swallowed, knowing she had allowed the situation to get out of hand and having little idea how to regain control. "Please, I've never been any good at handling this sort of thing, and..."

"What sort of thing is that?" he asked her. There was no lessening of his grip on her, no weakening in the strength of his eyes.

"Seth." Her pulse was beginning to beat wildly again. "Please, let me go in before I make a total fool of myself."

All the uncertainty of her emotions beamed from her eyes. She saw anger flash in his before he crushed her mouth in a swift, powerful kiss.

"Tomorrow," he said and released her.

Breathless, Lindsay ran her hand through her hair. "I think I'd better not...."

"Tomorrow," he said again before he turned and walked back to his car.

Lindsay watched its taillights disappear. *Tomorrow,* she thought and trembled once in the chill of the night air.

Chapter 6

Because she arose late, it was past noon before Lindsay finished her barre and changed. She was determined to keep her afternoon at the Cliff House casual and dressed accordingly in a rust-colored jogging suit. Tossing the matching jacket over her arm, Lindsay bounded down the stairs just as Carol Moorefield let herself in.

Mrs. Moorefield was as unlike her son as night and day. She was petite and slender, with sleek brunette hair and sophisticated looks that never seemed to age. Andy's looks came straight from his father, a man Lindsay had seen only in photographs, as Carol had been a widow for twenty years.

When her husband had died, she had taken over his florist business and had run it with style and a keen business sense. She was a woman whose opinion Lindsay valued and whose kindness she had grown to depend on.

"Looks like you're geared up to do some running," Carol commented as she closed the front door behind her. "I'd think you'd want to rest up after your date last night."

Lindsay kissed the lightly powdered cheek. "How'd you know I'd had a date? Did Mother call you?"

Carol laughed, running a hand down the length of Lindsay's hair. "Naturally, but I could have told her. Hattie MacDonald," she supplied with a jerk of her head to indicate the house across the street. "She saw him pick you up and gave me the early bulletin."

"How nice that I made the Saturday evening information exchange," Lindsay said dryly.

Carol turned into the living room to drop her purse and jacket on the sofa. "Did you have a nice time?"

"Yes, I...yes." Lindsay suddenly found it necessary to retie her tennis shoes. Carol studied the top of her head but said nothing. "We had dinner up the coast."

"What sort of man is he?"

Lindsay looked up, then slowly began to tie her other shoe. "I'm not completely sure," she murmured. "Interesting, certainly. Rather forceful and sure of himself, and just a little formal now and again, and yet..." She recalled his attitude toward Ruth. "And yet, I think he can be very patient, very sensitive."

Hearing the tone, Carol sighed. Though she, too, knew Lindsay was not for Andy, a tiny part of her heart still hoped. "You seem to like him."

"Yes..." The word came out in a long, thoughtful stretch. Laughing, Lindsay straightened. "At least, I think I do. Did you know he's S. N. Bannion, the architect?"

At the rate Carol's brows rose, Lindsay knew this was news. "Is he really? I thought he was going to marry some Frenchwoman, a race car driver."

"Apparently not."

"Well, this is interesting," Carol decided. She placed her hands on her hips as she did when she was truly impressed. "Does your mother know?"

"No, she…" Lindsay glanced back over her shoulder toward her mother's rooms. "No," she repeated, turning back. "I'm afraid I upset her last night. We haven't really spoken yet this morning."

"Lindsay." Carol touched her cheek, seeing the distress. "You mustn't let this sort of thing worry you."

Lindsay's eyes were suddenly wide and vulnerable. "I never seem to be able to do the right thing," she blurted out. "I owe her…"

"Stop it." Carol took her by the shoulders and gave them a brisk, no-nonsense shake. "It's ridiculous for children to go through life trying to pay back their parents. The only thing you owe Mae is love and respect. If you live your life trying to please someone else, you'll make two people unhappy. Now," she stroked Lindsay's hair again and smiled, "that's all the advice I have for today. I'm going to go talk Mae into a drive."

Lindsay threw her arms around Carol's neck and gave one desperate squeeze. "You're so good for us."

Pleased, Carol squeezed back. "Want to come?" she invited. "We can drive for awhile and have a fussy little lunch somewhere."

"No, I can't." She drew away. "Seth is picking me up soon to take me through his house."

"Ah, your Cliff House." Carol gave a knowledgeable nod. "This time you'll be able to wander about in broad daylight."

Lindsay grinned. "Do you think it'll lose some of its charm?"

"I doubt it." Carol turned to start down the hall. "Have fun, and don't worry about getting home to fix supper. Your mother and I will eat out." Before Lindsay could speak, the doorbell rang. "There's your young man," Carol announced and disappeared around the corner.

Lindsay turned to the door in a flurry of nerves. She had told herself that her response to Seth the night before had been abetted by the mood of the evening. It had been aided by her own lack of male companionship and his well-reported experience. It had been a moment only, nothing more. She told herself that now it was important to remember who he was and how easily he drew women. And how easily he left them.

It was important to channel their association into a careful friendship right from the outset. There was Ruth to think of. Lindsay knew that if she wanted what was right for Ruth, she had to keep her involvement with Ruth's uncle amicable. Like a business relationship, she decided, placing a hand on her stomach to quiet jarred nerves. Lightly friendly, no strings, nothing personal. Feeling herself settle, Lindsay opened the door.

He wore dark brown chinos and a bone-colored, crew-neck sweater. His raw physicality hit Lindsay instantly. She had known one or two other men who possessed this elemental sexual pull. Nick Davidov was one, and a choreographer she had worked with in the company was another. She recalled, too, that for them there had been women—never *a* woman—in their lives. Be careful, her brain flashed. *Be very careful.*

"Hi." Her smile was friendly, but the wariness was in her eyes. She slipped a small, canvas purse over her shoulder as she pulled the door shut behind her. Habitually, she offered her hand. "How are you?"

"Fine." With a slight pressure on her fingers, he stopped her from continuing down the porch steps. They stood almost precisely where they had stood the night before. Lindsay could all but feel the lingering energy in the air. Looking at him, she met one of his long, searching gazes. "How are you?"

"Fine," she managed, feeling foolish.

"Are you?" He was watching her carefully, deeply.

Lindsay felt her skin warm. "Yes, yes, of course I am." Annoyance replaced the guardedness in her eyes. "Why shouldn't I be?"

As if satisfied by her answer, Seth turned. Together they walked to his car. A strange man, Lindsay decided, unwittingly more intrigued than ever. Smiling, she shook her head. A very strange man.

As she started to slip into the car, she spotted three small birds chasing a crow across the sky. Amused, she followed their progress, listening to the taunting chatter. The crow arched toward the east and so did the trio of birds. Laughing, she turned, only to find herself in Seth's arms.

For a moment Lindsay lost everything but his face. Her being seemed to center on it. Her mouth warmed as his eyes lingered on hers. In invitation, her lips parted, her lids grew heavy. Abruptly she remembered what she had promised herself. Clearing her throat, she drew away. She settled herself in the car, then waited until she heard Seth shut the door before she let out a long, shaky breath.

She watched him move around the car to the driver's side. I'll have to start out in control of the situation and stay that way, she decided. She turned to him as he slid in beside her, and opted for bright conversation.

"Have you any idea how many eyes are trained on us at this moment?" she asked him.

Seth started the car but left it idling. "No, are there many?"

"Dozens." Though the car doors were closed, she lowered her voice conspiratorially. "Behind every curtain on the block. As you can see, I'm totally unaffected by the attention, but then, I'm a trained performer and used to center stage." Mischief was in her eyes. "I hope it doesn't make you nervous."

"Not a bit," Seth returned. In a quick move, he pinned her back against the seat, taking her mouth in a rapid, thrilling kiss. Though quick, it was thorough, leaving no portion of her mouth unexplored, no part of her system unaffected. When he drew away, Lindsay was breathing jerkily and staring. No one, she was certain, had ever felt what she was feeling at that moment.

"I hate to put on a dull show, don't you?" The words were low and intimate, stirring Lindsay's blood.

"Mmm," she answered noncommittally and slid cautiously away from him. This was not the way to stay in control.

The Cliff House was less than three miles from Lindsay's, but it stood high above the town, high above the rocks and water of the Sound. It was built of granite. To Lindsay's fascinated imagination, it seemed hewn from the cliff itself, carved out by a giant's hand. It was unrefined and fierce, a wicked castle perched at the very edge of the land. There were many chimneys, doors and windows, as the size of the place demanded them. But now, for the first time in more than a dozen years, Lindsay saw the house live. The windows sparkled, catching the sun, then holding it or tossing it back. There were no flowers yet to brighten the serious face of the house, but the lawn was neatly tended. And to her pleasure, there was smoke curling and drifting from the several chimneys The driveway was steep and long, starting out from the main road, curving along the way and ending at the front of the house.

"It's wonderful, isn't it?" Lindsay murmured. "I love the way it has its back turned to the sea, as if it isn't concerned with any power but its own."

Seth stopped the car at the end of the drive, then turned to her. "That's a rather fanciful thought."

"I'm a rather fanciful person."

"Yes, I know," Seth observed, and leaning across her, unlatched her door. He stayed close a moment so that the slightest move would have brought their mouths together. "Strangely, on you it's attractive. I've always preferred practical women."

"Have you?" Something seemed to happen to Lindsay when he was close. It was as if many threads, thin but impossibly strong, wound their way around her until she was helpless. "I've never been very good at practicalities. I'm better at dreaming."

He twisted the end of a strand of her hair around his fingers. "What sort of dreams?"

"Foolish ones mostly, I suppose. They're the best kind." Quickly she pushed the door open and stepped outside. Closing her eyes, she waited for her system to drift back to normal. When she heard his door shut, she opened them again to study the house. Casual, friendly, she reminded herself and took a deep breath.

"Do you know," she began, "the last time I walked here, it was about midnight and I was sixteen." She smiled, remembering, as they moved up the narrow walk toward a skirting porch. "I dragged poor Andy along and crawled through a side window."

"Andy." Seth paused at the front door. "That's the weight-lifter you were kissing in front of your studio."

Lindsay lifted a brow, acknowledging the description of Andy. She said nothing.

"Boyfriend?" Seth asked lightly, jiggling the keys in his palm as he studied her.

Lindsay kept her look bland. "I outgrew boyfriends a few years back, but he's a friend, yes."

"You're a very affectionate friend."

"Yes, I am," she agreed. "I've always considered the two words synonymous."

"An interesting outlook," Seth murmured and unlocked the door. "No need to crawl in a side window this time." He gestured her inside.

It was as awesome as Lindsay remembered. The ceilings in the entrance hall were twenty feet high with the rough beams exposed. A wide staircase curved to the left, then split in two and ran up opposing sides of an overhanging balcony. The banister was polished mirrorlike, and the treads were uncarpeted.

The dusty, peeling wallpaper Lindsay remembered had been stripped away to be replaced by a new fabric of rich cream. A long, narrow Persian carpet was spread on the oak-planked floor. The sun was muted, reflected on the prisms of a tiered chandelier.

Without speaking, she walked down the hall to the first doorway. The parlor had been completely restored. There was a bold floral print on one wall, offset by the lacquered pearl-colored tones of the others. Lindsay took a slow tour of the room. She stopped by a small, eighteenth-century table, touching it lightly with a fingertip.

"It's wonderful." She glanced at the thinly striped brocade of the sofa. "You knew precisely what was needed. I could almost have pictured this room with a Dresden shepherdess on the mantel—and there it is!" She walked over to study it, moved by its delicacy. "And French carpets on the floor...." Lindsay turned back with a smile that reflected all her pleasure with the room. Hers was a fragile, timeless beauty suited to the antiques and silks and brocades that now surrounded her. Seth took a step closer. Her perfume drifted to him. "Is Ruth here?" she asked.

"No, not at the moment." He surprised them both by reaching out to run a fingertip down her cheek. "She's at Monica's. This is the first time I've seen you with your hair down," he murmured, moving his fingers from her skin to her hair, where he tangled them in its length. "It suits you."

Lindsay felt the threads of desire reaching out for her and stepped back. "I had it down the first time we met." She smiled, ordering herself not to be foolish. "It was raining, as I remember."

Seth smiled back, first with his eyes, then with his lips. "So it was." He closed the distance between them again, then trailed a finger down her throat. Lindsay shivered involuntarily. "You're amazingly responsive," he said quietly. "Is that always true?"

Heat was rushing through her, pulsing where his flesh touched hers. Shaking her head, she turned away. "That's not a fair question."

"I'm not a fair man."

"No," Lindsay agreed and faced him again. "I don't think you are, at least not in your dealings with women. I came to see the house, Seth," she reminded him briskly. "Will you show it to me?"

He moved to her again but was suddenly interrupted. A small, trim man with a dark, silver-speckled beard appeared in the doorway. The beard was full, beautifully shaped, growing down from his ears to circle his mouth and cover his chin. It was all the more striking as it was the only hair on his head. He wore a black, three-piece suit with a crisp, white shirt and a dark tie. His posture was perfect, militarily correct, his hands at ease by his sides. Lindsay had an immediate impression of efficiency.

"Sir."

Seth turned to him, and the tension seemed to slip from the room. Lindsay's muscles relaxed. "Worth." He nodded in acknowledgement as he took Lindsay's arm. "Lindsay, Worth. Worth, Ms. Dunne."

"How do you do, miss?" The slight bow was European, the accent British. Lindsay was captivated.

"Hello, Mr. Worth." Her smile was spontaneously open and friendly as was the offering of her hand. Worth hesitated with a brief glance at Seth before accepting it. His touch was light, a bare brushing of her fingertips.

"You had a call, sir," he said, returning his attention to his

72

employer. "From Mr. Johnston in New York. He said it was quite important."

"All right, get him back for me. I'll be right in." He turned to Lindsay as Worth backed from the room. "Sorry, this shouldn't take long. Would you like a drink while you wait?"

"No." She glanced back to where Worth had stood. It was easier, she decided, to deal with Seth when he slipped into a formal attitude. Smiling, she wandered back to the window. "Go ahead, I'll just wait here."

With a murmur of assent, Seth left her.

It took less than ten minutes for Lindsay's curiosity to overpower her sense of propriety. This was a house she had explored in the dead of night when cobwebs and dust had been everywhere. It was impossible for her to resist exploring it when the sun was shining on a polished floor. She began to wander, intending to limit her tour to the main hall.

There were paintings to admire and a tapestry that took her breath away. On a table sat a Japanese tea set so thin, she thought it might shatter under her gaze. Too intrigued by the treasures she was discovering to remember her resolution to keep to the hall, she pushed open the door at the end of it and found herself in the kitchen.

It was a strange, appealing mixture of scrupulous efficiency and old-fashioned charm. The appliances were built-in, with stainless steel and chrome glistening everywhere. The counters were highly lacquered wood. The dishwasher hummed mechanically while a quiet little fire crackled in a waist-high hearth. Sunlight poured through the window illuminating the vinyl-covered walls and planked floors. Lindsay made a sound of pure appreciation.

Worth turned from his activity at a large butcher block table. He had removed his jacket, replacing it with a long, white, bibbed apron. An expression of astonishment ran across his face before he folded it into its habitual placid lines.

"May I help you, miss?"

"What a wonderful kitchen!" Lindsay exclaimed and let the door swing shut behind her. She turned a circle, smiling at the shining copper-bottomed kettles and pans that hung over Worth's head. "How clever Seth must be to have blended two worlds into one so perfectly."

"To be sure, miss," Worth agreed crisply. "Have you lost your way?" he asked and carefully wiped his hands on a cloth.

"No, I was just wandering a bit." Lindsay continued to do so around the kitchen while Worth stood correctly and watched her. "Kitchens are fascinating places, I think. The hub of the house, really. I've always regretted not learning to cook well."

She remembered the yogurts and salads of her professional dancing days, the occasional binges at an Italian or French restaurant, the rarely used refrigerator in her apartment. Eating had been something often overlooked in the crammed course of a day. Cooking had been out of the question.

"I'm baffled by anything more complex than a tuna casserole." She turned to Worth, still smiling. "I'm sure you're a marvelous cook." Lindsay stood just to the side of the window. The afternoon sun shone strong on her face, accentuating the fine bones and delicate complexion.

"I do my best, miss. Shall I serve you coffee in the parlor?"

Lindsay held back a sigh. "No, thank you, Mr. Worth. I suppose I'll just wander back and see if Seth is finished."

As she spoke, the door swung open and Seth walked through. "I'm sorry that took so long." The door closed soundlessly behind him.

"I barged into your kitchen without thinking." After casting a quick, apologetic glance at Worth, she moved to Seth. "Things have changed a bit since the last time I was here."

Some silent male message passed over her head between Seth and Worth before he took her arm to lead her through the door. "And you approve?"

She pushed her hair off her shoulder as she turned her face up to his. "I should reserve judgment until I see the rest, but I'm already captivated. And I *am* sorry," she continued, "about just walking into the kitchen that way. I got involved."

"Worth has a policy about women in the kitchen," Seth explained.

"Yes," Lindsay agreed wryly. "I think I know what the policy is. *Keep out.*"

"Very perceptive."

They moved through the downstairs rooms; the library, where the original paneling had been restored and polished to a glossy finish; a sitting room stripped of wallpaper and as yet unfinished; to Worth's quarters, spartan in cleanliness.

"The rest of the main level should be finished off this winter," Seth commented as they started up the staircase. Lindsay let her fingers trail over the banister. *How could wood feel this smooth?* she mused. "The house was solidly built, and there's generally only small bits of repair and redesigning to do," Seth continued.

The banister, she reflected, would have known the touch of countless palms and an occasional bottom. She grinned, thinking what a thrill it would be to slide all the way down from the third floor.

"You love this place," Seth stated, pausing at the landing, catching Lindsay between the banister and himself. They were close, and she tilted her head until she could meet his eyes. "Why?"

It was obvious he wanted an answer that was specific rather than general. Lindsay thought it through before speaking. "I think because it's always seemed so strong, so eternal. There's a fairy tale quality about it. Generation after generation, era after era, it endures."

Turning, Lindsay walked along the railing that overhung the first floor. Below, the line and space of the main hall ran parallel. "Do you think Ruth will adjust to living here? That she'll come to accept being settled in one place?"

"Why do you ask?"

Shrugging, Lindsay turned and began to walk with Seth down the hall. "Ruth interests me."

"Professionally."

"And personally," Lindsay countered, glancing up at his tone. "Are you against her dancing?"

He stopped at a doorway to fix her with one of his lengthy looks. "I'm not at all certain your definition of dancing and mine are the same."

"Maybe not," she acknowledged. "But perhaps Ruth's definition would be more to the point."

"She's very young. And," he added before Lindsay could retort, "my responsibility." Opening the door, he guided her inside.

The room was unmistakably feminine. Pale blue Priscilla curtains fluttered at the windows, and the shade was repeated in the counterpane. There was a white brick fireplace with a brass fan-shaped screen in front of the hearth. English ivy trailed from a brass pot on a piecrust table. Lining the walls were framed pictures of ballet stars. Lindsay saw the poster Seth had spoken of. Her Juliet to Davidov's Romeo. Memories flooded back.

"There's no doubt about whose room this is," she murmured, glancing at the pink satin ribbons on the bureau. She looked up to study Seth's chiseled features. He is a man, accustomed to seeing things exclusively from a man's perspective, she realized. He could easily have settled Ruth in a boarding school and sent her generous checks. Had it been difficult to make room for a girl and a girl's unique needs in his life?

"Are you a generous man on the whole, Seth," she asked curiously, "or is it selective?"

She saw his brow lift. "You have a habit of asking unusual questions." Taking her arm, he began to lead her back down the hall.

"And you've a talent for evading them."

"This is the room that should interest your ghost," Seth smoothly changed the subject.

Lindsay waited for Seth to open the door, then stepped inside. "Oh, yes!" She walked to the center and turned a quick circle. Her hair followed in a slow arch. "It's perfect."

Deep, curved window seats were cushioned in burgundy velvet, the shade picked up in the pattern of a huge Oriental rug. The furniture was old, heavy Victorian, gleaming from Worth's attentiveness. Nothing could have suited the high, wide room more. There was a blanket chest at the foot of the four-poster bed and pewter candlesticks on either side table.

"It's because you're an architect, I suppose," Lindsay said, admiringly. "You seem to know exactly what's needed."

The fireplace was stone and massive, sending images of thundering flames through Lindsay's mind. On a long, dark night the fire would roar, then crackle, then sizzle as the hours passed. She had a vivid flash of herself curled in the huge bed with Seth's body warming hers. A bit stunned by the clarity of the vision, she turned to wander about the room.

Too soon, she told herself. *Too fast.* Remember who he is. Silently she juggled the unexpected and unwanted emotions. At the French doors she paused, pushing them both open to step out. A rush of wind met her.

There was the raw sound of water against rock, the scent of salt in the chilling air. Lindsay watched the clouds scrambling across the sky chased by the wild wind. She walked to the rail and looked down. The drop was sheer and deadly. The fierce waves battered the jagged rocks, receding only to gather force to strike again. Lost in the wild excitement of the scene, Lindsay was not fully aware of Seth close behind her. When he turned her toward him, her response was as unrestrained and inevitable as the moving clouds above, the pounding surf below.

Her arms reached up to circle his neck as he drew her close. They came together. Her mouth molded to his, the hunger instant. She didn't hesitate but answered the intimacies of the kiss, exploring with her tongue until his taste mixed with hers. When he touched her, she trembled, not from fear or resistance, but from pure pleasure.

His hand slid under her shirt, trailing briefly along her ribcage. He cupped her breast; she was small and his hand was large. Slowly, while he took the kiss deeper, he traced his finger over the swell. As she had longed to do, she tangled her fingers in his hair. There was an impossible surge of need. It ran through her quickly—a river changing course. The current was irresistible, dragging her along into more turbulent waters. His fingers warmed against her skin as they roamed, spreading waves of delight.

When he took his mouth from hers to ravage the cord of her neck, Lindsay felt her body suffused by a sudden heat. The chill of the wind was a shock to her face and only increased the excitement. His teeth brought tiny ripples of pain to blend with the pleasure. The sound of the surf echoed in her brain, but through it she heard him murmur her name. When his mouth returned to claim hers, she welcomed it eagerly. Never had desire been so quick, so all-consuming.

Seth tore his mouth from hers, bringing his hands to her shoulders to keep her close. His eyes locked on hers. In them, Lindsay recognized anger and passion. A fresh tremor of excitement sped up her spine. She would have melted back into his arms had he not held her away.

"I want you." The wind tossed his hair around his face. His brows were lowered, accentuating the slight upsweep at the tips.

Lindsay could hear her heartbeat increase to roar in her brain like the waves below. She was courting danger and knew it, but the extent of it began to seep through. "No." She shook her head even as she felt the flush of desire on her cheeks. "No." The ground was unsteady under her feet. She moved away to grip the rail and breathe deep of the cold, sea air. It left her throat raw and tingling. Abruptly, Seth took her arm and spun her around.

"What the hell do you mean, no?" His voice was deadly low.

Lindsay shook her head again. The wind threw her hair into her eyes, and she tossed it back, wanting to see him clearly. Something in his stance was as untamed and fierce as the surf below them. This was the volcano. It drew her, tempted her. "Just that," she said. "What happened just now was unavoidable, but it won't go beyond that."

Seth came closer. A strong hand took hold of the back of her neck. Lindsay could feel the weight and texture of each separate finger. "You don't believe that."

His mouth lowered swiftly to hers, but instead of demand, he used persuasion. He traced his tongue between her lips until they parted on a sigh. He plundered, but gently, devastatingly. Lindsay gripped his arms to keep her balance. Her breath was as trapped as it would have been had she tumbled over the edge of the balcony to cartwheel through the air to the rocks below.

"I want to make love with you." The movement of his lips against hers shot an ache of desire through her. Lindsay struggled away.

For a moment she didn't speak but stood, catching her breath and watching him. "You have to understand," she began, then paused for her voice to steady. "You have to understand the kind of person I am. I'm not capable of casual affairs or one-night stands." Again she tossed her hair from her eyes. "I need more than that. I haven't your sophistication, Seth, I can't—I won't—compete with the women you've had in your life."

She turned to move away, but he took her arm again, keeping her facing toward him. "Do you really think we can walk away from what's already between us?"

"Yes." The word came out sharply as doubts crowded her. "It's necessary."

"I want to see you tonight."

"No, absolutely not." He was close, and Lindsay backed away.

"Lindsay, I'm not going to let this pass."

She shook her head. "The only thing between us is Ruth. Things would be simpler if we'd both remember that."

"Simple?" He caught a strand of her hair. A half-smile played around his mouth. "I don't think you're the sort of woman who'd be satisfied with simplicity."

"You don't know me," she retorted.

He smiled fully now, and releasing her hair, took her arm to lead her firmly into the house. "Perhaps not, Lindsay," he agreed pleasantly, "but I will." The iron determination of his tone was not lost on Lindsay.

Chapter 7

It had been almost a month since Ruth had joined Lindsay's school. The weather had turned cold quickly, and already there was a hint of snow in the air. Lindsay did her best to keep the school's ancient furnace operating to its fullest capacity. With a shirt tied loosely at the waist over her leotard, she taught the final class of the day.

"Glissade, glissade. Arabesque on *pointe."* As she spoke, Lindsay moved up and down the line of students, watching each critically for form and posture. She was pleased with her advanced *pointe* class. The students were good, possessing a firm understanding of music and movement. But the longer Ruth remained in the class, the more she stood apart from the others.

Her talent is so far above the ordinary, Lindsay thought, studying her for posture and flow. *She's being wasted here.* The now-familiar frustration overcame her, bordering on anger. And the look in her eyes, she thought as she signaled to one of the girls to keep her chin lifted, says, *"I want."* How do I convince Seth to let her go for it—and to let her go for it now before it slips away?

At the thought of Seth, Lindsay's attention wavered from her students. It locked on the last time she had seen him. If she were honest with herself, she'd admit that she'd thought of him over and over again these past weeks. She wanted to tell herself that the physical attraction she felt for him would fade. But remembering the strength, remembering the speed, she knew it was a lie.

"*Tendu,*" Lindsay instructed and folded her arms over her chest. Still the memories of his touch, of his taste, lingered. Often she had caught herself wondering what he was doing—when she was drinking coffee in the morning, when she was alone in the studio in the evening, when she woke without cause in the middle of the night. And she had forced herself to resist the urge to question Ruth.

I will not make a fool of myself over this man, she thought.

"Brenda, hands." Lindsay demonstrated, fingers flowing with a movement of her wrist. The ringing of the phone caught her by surprise. She gave her watch a frown. No one ever called the studio during class. Instantly the thought rushed through her mind: *Mother.*

"Take over, Brenda." Without waiting for a reply, she raced back to her office and grabbed the phone.

"Yes, Cliffside School of Dance." Her heart fluttered in her throat.

"Lindsay? Lindsay, is that you?"

"Yes, I..." Her hand paused on its way to her lips. "Nicky." There was no mistaking the musical Russian accent. "Oh, Nick, how wonderful to hear your voice!" Monica's piano playing continued smoothly. Lindsay cupped her hand over her ear as she sat. "Where are you?"

"In New York, of course." There was a laughing lilt to his voice which she had always loved. "How is your school progressing?"

"Very well. I've worked with some very good dancers. In fact, there's one in particular I want badly to send up to you. She's special, Nick, beautifully built, and..."

"Later, later." As he cut off Lindsay's enthusiastic report of Ruth, she could almost see the quick brushing-away gesture that would have accompanied the words. "I've called to talk about you. Your mother does well?"

Lindsay's hesitation was barely a sigh. "Much better. She's been getting around on her own for some time now."

"Good. Very good. Then when are you coming back?"

"Nick." Lindsay moved her shoulders, then glanced at the wall at the photograph of herself dancing with the man on the other end of the phone. Three years, she mused. It might as well be thirty. "It's been too long, Nick."

"Nonsense. You're needed."

She shook her head. He had always been dictatorial. Perhaps, she thought, it's my fate to tangle with domineering men. "I'm not in shape, Nick, not for the merry-go-round. There's young talent coming up." Her mind drifted back to Ruth. "*They're* needed."

"Since when are you afraid of hard work and competition?"

The challenge in his voice was an old ruse that made Lindsay smile. "We're both aware that teaching dance for three years is entirely different from performing for three years. Time doesn't stand still, Nick, not even for you."

"Afraid?"

"Yes. A little, yes."

He laughed at the confession. "Good, the fear will push you to dance better." He broke in on her exasperated laugh. "I need you, *ptichka,* my little bird. I've almost finished writing my first ballet."

"Nick, that's wonderful! I had no idea you were working on anything."

"I have another year, perhaps two, to dance. I have no interest in character parts." During the slight pause, Lindsay heard the murmur of girls as they changed into their outdoor shoes. "I've been offered the directorship of the company."

"I can't say I'm surprised," Lindsay returned warmly. "But I am pleased, for you and for them."

"I want you back, Lindsay, back in the company. It can be arranged, you know, with some strings pulled."

"I don't want that. No, I..."

"There is no one to dance my ballet but you. She is Ariel, and Ariel is you."

"Oh, Nick, please." Lifting a hand, she pinched the bridge of her nose between her thumb and forefinger. She had put the world he was offering behind her.

"No, no argument, not over the phone." She shook her head silently and shut her eyes. "When I've finished the ballet, I'm coming to Cliffdrop."

"Cliffside," Lindsay corrected. She opened her eyes as a smile came to her lips.

"Side, drop, I'm Russian. It's expected. I'll be there in January," he continued, "to show you the ballet. Then you'll come back with me."

"Nick, you make it sound so simple."

"Because it is, *ptichka*. In January."

Lindsay took the dead receiver from her ear and stared at it. How like Nick, she mused. He was famous for his grand, impulsive gestures, his total dedication to the dance. And he's so brilliant, she thought, replacing the receiver. So confident. He'd never understand that some things can be tucked away in a memory box and still remain precious and alive. For Nick it was all so simple.

She rose and walked over to study the photograph. It's the company first, last and always. But for me there are so many other factors, so many other needs. I don't even know what they are, only that I have them. She folded her arms across her chest, hugging her

84

elbows. Maybe this was the time of decision. A flutter of impatience ran through her. I've been coasting for too long, she accused. Shaking herself back to the moment, Lindsay walked into the studio. Students were still milling about, reluctant to leave the warmth of the school for the cold outside. Ruth had returned to the barre alone to practice. In the mirror, her eyes followed Lindsay across the room. Monica looked up with her cheerful smile.

"Ruth and I are going to do a pizza and a movie. Want to come?"

"Sounds great, but I want to do a little more work on the staging for *The Nutcracker*. Christmas will be here before we know it."

Monica reached out to touch her hand. "You work too hard, Lindsay."

Lindsay squeezed Monica's hand, meeting the grave, concerned eyes. "I've just been giving that some thought." Both women glanced up as the door opened. A blast of cold air whooshed in with Andy. His normally pale complexion was reddened with cold, his huge shoulders hunched against it.

"Hi!" Lindsay held out her hands to take both of his. She chafed at the chill. "I didn't expect to see you tonight."

"Looks as though I timed it pretty well." He gave a quick look around as students pulled slacks and sweaters over their leotards. He greeted Monica casually; she, in turn, seemed to nod almost hopefully in Andy's direction.

"Hello, Andy," she seemed to stammer at last.

Ruth watched the simple exchange from across the room. It was so obvious, she thought, to everyone but the three of them. He was crazy in love with Lindsay, and Monica was crazy in love with him. She had seen Monica flush with anticipation the moment Andy had entered the studio. He, on the other hand, had seen only Lindsay. How strange people are, she reflected as she executed a *grand plié*.

And Lindsay. Lindsay was everything Ruth ever hoped to be: a true ballerina, confident, poised, beautiful, with something elusive in her movements. Ruth thought she moved not like a butterfly or bird, but like a cloud. There was something light, something free, in each step, in each gesture. It wasn't with envy that Ruth watched her, but with longing. And she did watch her, closely, continually. And because she did so, Ruth felt she was growing to know Lindsay well.

Ruth admired Lindsay's openness, her free flow of emotions. She had warmth, which drew people to her. But there was more playing beneath the surface, much more, Ruth felt, than Lindsay was in the habit of revealing. Ruth doubted whether those hidden passions were often fully released. It would take something strong, like the dance itself, to release them.

As Ruth pondered these thoughts, the door opened again, and her uncle strode into the studio.

A smile sprang to Ruth's lips along with a greeting. She halted the latter to play the observer once more.

The jolt of the eye contact between Seth and Lindsay was quick and volcanic. Its flare was so short that had she not been watching so intensely, she would have missed it. But it was real and potent. She paused a moment, frowning thoughtfully at her mentor and her uncle. This was unexpected, and she didn't know how she felt about it. The attraction between them was as patently obvious to her as Monica's for Andy and Andy's for Lindsay.

Amazing, she decided, that none of them seemed aware of the emotions at play among the four of them. She remembered the awareness in her parents' eyes when they had looked at each other. The vision brought both warmth and sadness. Ruth badly wanted to feel a part of that kind of love again. Without speaking, she moved to the corner of the room to remove her toe shoes.

* * *

The moment Lindsay had looked over and seen Seth, she had felt the power. It flooded her, then ebbed so swiftly she was certain that her legs had dissolved below the knees. No, the attraction hadn't faded. It had doubled. Everything about him was instantly implanted in her brain: his wind-tousled hair, the way he left his sheepskin jacket unbuttoned to the cold, the way his eyes seemed to swallow her the moment he stepped inside.

It seemed impossible that without even an effort she could completely obliterate everyone else from her consciousness. They might have stood alone, on an island, on a mountaintop, so complete was her absorption with him.

I've missed him, she realized abruptly. *It's been twenty-six days since I've seen him, spoken to him. A month ago I didn't know he existed, and now I think about him at all sorts of odd, unexpected times.* Her smile began of its own volition. Though Seth didn't return it, Lindsay stepped forward, extending her hands.

"Hello. I've missed seeing you."

The statement came spontaneously and without guile. She took Seth's hands as he studied her face.

"Have you?" He asked the question quietly, but the demand in his tone reminded Lindsay to use caution.

"Yes," she admitted. She took her hands from his and turned. "You know Monica and Andy, don't you?" Monica stood near the piano stacking sheet music, but Lindsay approached her now and claimed the task. "You don't have to bother with that," she said. "You and Ruth must be starving, and you'll miss that movie if you stay around too long." She rambled, annoyed with herself. *Why,* she asked herself, *don't I ever think before I speak?* She lifted her hand in farewell as loitering students trickled out. "Have you eaten, Andy?"

87

"Well, no, actually, that's why I stopped by." He glanced at Seth. "I thought maybe you'd like to grab a hamburger and take in a movie."

"Oh, Andy, that's sweet." She stopped shuffling music to smile at him. "But I've got some work to finish up. I've just turned down a similar offer from Monica and Ruth. Why don't you switch to pizza and go with them?"

"Sure, Andy." Monica spoke up rapidly, then struggled with a flush. "That'd be fun, wouldn't it, Ruth?"

At the entreaty in Monica's liquid brown eyes, Ruth smiled and nodded. "You weren't coming by for me, were you, Uncle Seth?" Ruth rose, pulling on jeans.

"No." He watched his niece's head disappear inside a bulky sweater, then pop through the neck opening. "I came to have a few words with Lindsay."

"Well, we should get out of your way." Monica moved with a grace unexpected in a large-boned girl. There was an athletic swing to her gait softened by her own early years at the barre. Grabbing her coat, she looked back at Andy. Her smile wasn't reserved, but hesitant. "Coming, Andy?" She saw the quick glance he aimed at Lindsay. Her heart sank.

"Sure." He touched Lindsay's shoulder. "See you tomorrow."

"Night, Andy." Rising on her toes, she gave him a light kiss. "Have a good time." The statement was made to all three. Andy and Monica walked to the door, both battling depression. Ruth trailed after them, a smile lurking at her mouth.

"Good night, Uncle Seth, Ms. Dunne." She pulled the studio door firmly shut behind her.

Lindsay stared at the closed panel a moment, wondering what had caused the gleam in Ruth's eyes. It had been mischief, pure and simple, and though it pleased her to see it, Lindsay wondered at its cause. Shaking her head, she turned back to Seth.

"Well," she began brightly, "I suppose you want to discuss Ruth. I think…"

"No."

Lindsay's thoughts paused in midstream, then backed up. "No?" she repeated. Her expression was one of genuine bafflement until Seth took a step closer. Then she understood. "We really should talk about her." Turning away, she wandered to the room's center. In the wall of mirrors, she could see their reflections. "She's far more advanced than any of my other students, far more dedicated, far more talented. Some were born to dance, Seth. Ruth is one of them."

"Perhaps." Casually, he shrugged out of his jacket and laid it on top of the piano. She knew instinctively that tonight he wouldn't be easy to deal with. Her fingers plucked at the knot in her shirt. "But it's been one month, not six. We'll talk about Ruth next summer."

"That's absurd." Annoyed, Lindsay turned to face him. It was a mistake, she discovered, as the reality of him was far more potent than the mirror image. She turned away again and began to pace quickly. "You make it sound as though this is a whim she'll outgrow. That's simply unrealistic. She's a dancer, Seth. Five months from now she'll still be a dancer."

"Then waiting shouldn't be a problem."

His logic caused Lindsay to close her eyes in a spurt of fury. She wanted badly to reason with him calmly. "Wasted time," she said with quiet control. "And in this situation, wasted time is a sin. She needs more—so much more—than I can give her here."

"She needs stability first." There was annoyance just under the surface of his voice. It mirrored Lindsay's own sentiments as the glass did their bodies.

"She has something," she tossed back, gesturing with both arms in frustration. "Why do you refuse to see it? It's rare and beautiful, but it needs to be nurtured, it needs to be disciplined. It only becomes more difficult to do that as time goes on."

"I told you before, Ruth's my responsibility." His voice had sharpened to a fine edge. "And I told you I didn't come to discuss Ruth. Not tonight."

Lindsay's intuition repressed her retort. She'd get nowhere with him now, not this way, and it was possible to ruin the chance of any further opportunity. To win for Ruth, she needed patience.

"All right." She took a deep breath and felt her temper recede. "Why did you come?"

He walked to her, taking her firmly by the shoulders before she could move away. "You missed seeing me?" he asked as his eyes bored into hers in the glass.

"In a small town like this it's rare to go nearly a month without seeing someone." She tried to step away, but his fingers tightened.

"I've been working on a project, a medical center to be built in New Zealand. The drawings are nearly finished now."

Because the idea intrigued her, Lindsay relaxed. "How exciting that must be—to create something out of your head that people will walk in, live in, work in. Something that's solid and lasting. Why did you become an architect?"

"Buildings fascinated me." He began a slow massage of her shoulders, but her interest was focused on his words. "I wondered why they were built in certain ways, why people chose different styles. I wanted to make them functional and appealing to the eye." His thumb trailed up the nape of her neck and awakened a myriad of nerve endings. "I've a weakness for beauty." Slowly, while Lindsay's eyes were glued to the mirror, he lowered his mouth to tease the freshly aroused skin. A breath trembled through her lips to be sucked back in at the contact.

"Seth..."

"Why did you become a dancer?" His question interrupted her protest. He kneaded her muscles with his fingers and watched her in the mirror. He caught the desire flickering in her eyes.

"It was all there ever was for me." Lindsay's words were husky, clouded with restrained passion. She found it hard to concentrate on her own words. "My mother spoke of nothing else as far back as I can remember."

"So you became a dancer for her." He lifted a hand to her hair and drew out a pin.

"No, some things are meant to be. This was meant for me." His hand trailed up the side of her neck to bury itself in her hair. He drew out another pin. "It would have been dancing for me regardless of my mother. She only made it more important sooner. What are you doing?" She placed a hand over his as he began to withdraw another pin.

"I like your hair down, where I can feel it."

"Seth, don't..."

"You always wear it up when you're teaching, don't you?"

"Yes, I..." The weight of her hair pushed against the remaining pins until they fell to the floor. Her hair tumbled free in pale blond clouds.

"School's out," he murmured, then buried his face in its thickness.

Their reflection showed her the sharp contrast of his hair against hers, of his tanned fingers against the ivory skin of her throat. There was a magic about watching him brush the hair from her neck and lower his mouth while feeling his lips and fingers on her skin. Fascinated, she watched the couple in the wall of the mirrors. When he turned her so that flesh and blood faced flesh and blood, she felt no lessening of the trance. Totally involved, she stared up at him.

He lowered his mouth, and though her lips hungered, he feathered kisses along her jawline. His hands moved greedily through her hair while he teased her face with promising kisses. Lindsay began to burn for the intimacy that comes with the joining of mouth to mouth. But even as she turned her head to find his lips, he drew her away.

Waves of heat rose from her toes, concentrating in her lungs until she was certain they would explode from the pleasure. With his eyes locked on hers, Seth slowly untied the knot in her shirt. Barely touching her, he ran his fingers up her shoulders, lingering only a heartbeat away from the swell of her breasts. Gently, he pushed the shirt from her until it drifted soundlessly to the floor.

There was something stunningly sexual in the gesture. Lindsay felt naked before him. He had destroyed all her barricades. There was no longer room for illusions. Stepping forward, she rose on her toes to take his mouth with hers.

The kiss started slowly, luxuriously, with the patience of two people who know the pleasure they can bring to each other. The mouth is for tasting, and they assuaged a hunger that had grown sharp and deep with fasting. They supped without hurry, as if wanting to prolong the moment of full contentment.

Lindsay took her lips from his to explore. There was a hint of roughness at his jawline from the day's growth of beard. His cheekbones were long and close to his skin. Below his ear his taste was mysteriously male. She lingered there, savoring it.

His hands were on her hips, and his fingers trailed along the tops of her thighs. She shifted so that he might touch her more freely. On a long, gradual journey, he brought his hand to her breast. Her leotard was snug, hardly an intrusion between his palm and her flesh.

Their lips joined in a hot, desperate demand as their bodies strained, one against the other. His arms swept her closer, nearly bringing her off the floor. There was no longer comfort, no longer leisure, but the pain was exquisite.

As from down a long tunnel, Lindsay heard the ringing of the bell. She burrowed deeper into Seth. The ringing came again, and yet again, until its meaning sunk into her consciousness. She moved against him, but he caught her closer.

"Let it ring, damn it." His mouth took hers, swallowing the words.

"Seth, I can't." Lindsay struggled through the mists in her brain. "I can't...my mother."

He swore richly but loosened his hold. Pushing away, Lindsay rushed to answer the phone.

"Yes?" Passing a hand through her hair, she tried to gather enough of her wits to remember where she was.

"Miss Dunne?"

"Yes. Yes, this is Lindsay Dunne." She sat on the corner of her desk as her knees trembled.

"I'm sorry to disturb you, Miss Dunne. This is Worth. Might I find Mr. Bannion there?"

"Worth?" Lindsay slowly let air in and out of her lungs. "Oh, yes. Yes, he's here. Just a moment."

Her movements were slow and deliberate as she set the receiver beside the phone and rose. For a moment she stood in the doorway of her office. He was turned toward her, and his eyes met hers instantly as if he'd been waiting for her return. Lindsay stepped into the studio, resisting the need to clasp her hands together.

"It's for you," she told him. "Mr. Worth."

Seth nodded, but there was nothing casual in the way he took her shoulders as he passed. Briefly, they stood side by side. "I'll only be a moment."

Lindsay remained still until she heard the murmur of his voice on the phone. Whenever she finished a difficult dance, she always took a few moments to breathe. It was concentrated breathing, in-out, deep and slow, not the unconscious movement of air in the lungs. She took time to do so now. Gradually, she felt the flow of blood decrease, the hammer of her pulse quiet. The tingle just under her skin faded. Satisfied that her body was responding, Lindsay waited for her mind to follow suit.

Even for a woman who enjoyed taking risks, Lindsay knew the idiocy of her behavior. With Seth Bannion, the odds were too highly stacked against her. She was beginning to realize that she contributed to those odds. She was too attracted to him, too vulnerable to him. It didn't seem to matter that she had known him for only a matter of weeks.

Slowly, she walked to the shirt that lay on the floor. She stooped just as a movement in the mirror caught her eye. Again, her eyes locked with Seth's in the glass. Chilled pinpricks spread over her skin. Lindsay rose and turned. Now, she knew, was not the time for fantasies and illusions.

"A problem on a site," he said briefly. "I need to check some figures at home." He crossed to her, "Come with me."

There was no mistaking what he meant. To Lindsay, the simplicity and directness were overpoweringly seductive. With careful movements, she slipped back into her shirt.

"No, I can't. I've work to do, and then..."

"Lindsay." He halted her with a word and a hand to her cheek. "I want to sleep with you. I want to wake up with you."

She let out a long breath. "I'm not accustomed to dealing with this sort of thing," she murmured. She ran a hand through her loosened hair, then her eyes lifted to his again and held. "I'm very attracted to you. It's a bit beyond what I've felt before and I don't know quite what to do about it."

Seth's hand moved from her cheek to circle her throat. "Do you think you can tell me that and expect me to go home alone?"

Lindsay shook her head and put a decisive hand to his chest. "I tell you that, I suppose, because I'm not sophisticated enough to keep it to myself. I don't believe in lies and pretense." A faint line appeared between her brows as she continued. "And I don't believe in doing something I'm not totally sure is what I want. I'm not going to sleep with you."

"But you are." He put his hand over hers, capturing the other at the same time. "If not tonight, tomorrow; if not tomorrow, the day after."

"I wouldn't be so smug if I were you." Lindsay shook off his hands. "I'm never very obliging when told what I'm going to do. I make my own decisions."

"And you made this one," Seth said easily, but temper flared in his eyes. "The first time I kissed you. Hypocrisy doesn't suit you."

"Hypocrisy?" Lindsay held the words back a moment, knowing she would stutter. "The precious male ego! Refuse a proposition and you're a hypocrite."

"I don't believe *proposition* is a fully accurate term."

"Go sit on your semantics," she invited. "And do it elsewhere. I've got work to do."

He was quick. He grabbed her arm, jerking her against him before the command to step away could shoot from her brain to her feet. "Don't push me, Lindsay."

She pulled at her arm. It remained in his grip. "Aren't you the one who's pushing?"

"It appears we have a problem."

"*Your* problem," she tossed back. "I'm not going to be another set of blueprints in your file. If I decide I want to go to bed with you, I'll let you know. In the meantime, our main topic of conversation is Ruth."

Seth made an intense study of her face. Her cheeks had flushed with temper, her breath came quickly. A hint of a smile played on his mouth. "Right now you look a bit as you did when I watched you dance Dulcinea, full of passion and spirit. We'll talk again." Before Lindsay could comment, he gave her a long, lingering kiss. "Soon."

She managed to gather her wits as he crossed to the piano to retrieve his jacket. "About Ruth..."

He shrugged into his coat, all the time watching her. "Soon," he repeated and strode to the door.

Chapter 8

On Sundays Lindsay had no set schedule. Six days a week her time was regimented, given over to classes and paperwork and her mother. On Sunday she broke free.

It was late morning when she wandered downstairs. The aroma of coffee was strong, drawing her into the kitchen. She could hear her mother's slow, uneven movements before she pushed open the door.

"Morning." Lindsay crossed the linoleum floor to kiss Mae's cheek, then studied her neat, three-piece suit. "You're all dressed up." Pleasure warmed her voice. "You look wonderful."

Mae smiled as she touched her hair with a fussy hand. "Carol wanted to have lunch at the country club. Do you think my hair's all right?"

"It's lovely." Lindsay's heart lightened as she watched her mother preen again. "But you know it's your legs everybody looks at. You've got great legs."

Mae laughed, a sound Lindsay had waited a long time to hear. "Your father always thought so." The tone was sad again. Lindsay slipped her arms around Mae's neck.

"No, don't, please." She held her close a moment, willing away the gloom. "It's so good to see you smile. Dad would want you to smile." When she felt Mae sigh, she held her closer. If it were possible, she would have transfused some of her own strength into her. Mae patted Lindsay's back, then drew away.

"Let's have coffee." She moved to sit at the table. "My legs might look good, but they're still attached to this hip, and they get tired easily."

Lindsay watched as her mother carefully settled herself, then turned to the cupboard. It was important to keep Mae's mood on the upswing. "I worked late yesterday with the girl I've been telling you about, Ruth Bannion." Lindsay poured two cups of coffee before walking to the refrigerator for milk. She added a generous dose to her mother's and left her own black. "She's exceptional, truly exceptional," she continued as she walked over to join Mae. "I've cast her as Carla in *The Nutcracker*. She's a shy, introverted girl who seems really confident only when she's dancing." Thoughtfully, Lindsay watched the steam curl up from the surface of her coffee. "I want to send her to New York, to Nick. Her uncle won't even discuss it." Not for four and a half more months, she thought grimly. Stubborn, immovable... "Are all men mules?" Lindsay demanded, then swore as she scalded her tongue with a sip of steaming coffee.

"For the most part," Mae told her. Her own coffee sat cooling in front of her. "And for the most part, women seem to be attracted to mules. You're attracted to him."

Lindsay glanced up, then stared back down at the coffee. "Well...yes. He's a bit different from the men I've known. His life doesn't center around dancing. He's traveled almost everywhere. He's very sure of himself and arrogant in a very controlled sort of way. The only other man I've known who has that sort of confidence is Nick." She smiled, remembering, and her hands floated with the words. "But Nicky has that passionate Russian temper. He throws things, he moans, he shrieks. Even his moods are elaborately orchestrated. Seth is different. Seth would just quietly snap you in two."

"And you respect him for that."

Lindsay looked up again, then laughed. It was the first time she remembered she and her mother having an in-depth discussion on anything that didn't directly involve dancing. "Yes," she agreed. "As ridiculous as it sounds, I do. He's the sort of man who commands respect without demanding it, if you know what I mean." Lindsay sipped her coffee with more caution. "Ruth adores him. It shows in her face whenever she looks at him. The lonely look is fading from her eyes and I'm sure it's his doing." Her voice softened. "He's very sensitive, I think, and very much in control of his emotions. I think if he loved someone, he'd be very demanding because he wouldn't invest his emotions easily. Still, if he weren't so stubborn, I'd send Ruth to Nick. A year's training in New York, and I'm sure she'd be chosen for the *corps*. I mentioned her to him, but..."

"To Nick?" Mae interrupted Lindsay's verbal thoughts. "When?"

She brought herself back with a mental curse. It hadn't been an oversight that she had neglected to mention Nick's call. She had wanted to avoid a topic that brought pain to both of them. Now she shrugged and spoke casually between sips. "Oh, a couple of days ago. He called the studio."

"Why?"

Mae's question was quiet and unavoidable. "To see how I was, to ask after you." The flowers Carol had brought the week before were wilting in the bowl on the table. She rose, taking them with her. "He was always very fond of you."

Mae watched her daughter as she tossed the faded flowers into the trash. "He asked you to come back."

Lindsay placed the bowl in the sink and began to rinse it. "He's excited about a new ballet he's written."

"And he wants you for it." Lindsay continued to rinse the bowl. "What did you tell him?"

She shook her head, wanting only to avoid another strained argument. "Mother, please."

There was silence for a moment with only the sound of water splashing in the sink. It warmed Lindsay's hands.

"I've been thinking I might go to California with Carol."

Surprised by both the statement and the calm tone of her mother's voice, Lindsay turned without switching off the faucet. "That would be wonderful for you. You'd miss the worst of the winter."

"Not for the winter," Mae countered. "Permanently."

"Permanently?" Lindsay's face clouded with confusion. Behind her the water danced against the glass bowl. Reaching back, she twisted the handle of the faucet. "I don't understand."

"She has people there, you know." Mae rose to get more coffee, motioning a protest as Lindsay moved to do it for her. "One of them, a cousin, found a florist who was selling out. Good location. Carol bought it."

"She bought it?" Astonished, Lindsay sat down again. "But when? She hasn't said a word. Andy hasn't said anything either; I just saw him...."

"She wanted everything settled first." Mae interrupted Lindsay's disbelief. "She wants me to be her partner."

"Her partner?" Lindsay shook her head, then pressed fingers to both temples. "In California?"

"We can't go on this way, Lindsay." Mae limped back to the table with her coffee. "Physically, I'm as good as I'm going to be. There's no need for me to be pampered or for you to worry about me anymore. Yes, you do," she continued, even as Lindsay opened her mouth to object. "I'm a long way from where I was when I came out of the hospital."

"I know. I know that, but California...." She sent Mae a helpless look. "It's so far away."

"It's what we both need. Carol told me I was pressuring you, and she's right."

"Mother..."

"No, I do, and I'll keep right on doing it as long as we're living in each other's pockets this way." After a long breath, Mae pursed her lips. "It's time...for both of us. I've only wanted one thing for you. I haven't stopped wanting it." She took Lindsay's hands, studying the long, graceful fingers. "Dreams are stubborn things. I've had the same one all my life...first for me, then for you. Maybe that's wrong. Maybe you're using me as an excuse not to go back." Even as Lindsay shook her head, she continued. "You took care of me when I needed you, and I'm grateful. I haven't shown it always because the dream got in the way. I'm going to ask you something one last time." Lindsay remained silent, waiting. "Think about what you have, who you are. Think about going back."

There was nothing Lindsay could do but nod. She had thought about it, long and painfully two years before, but she wouldn't shut the door between herself and her mother; it had just worked its way open. "When would you go?"

"In three weeks."

Letting out a quick breath at the reply, Lindsay rose. "You and Carol will make great partners." She suddenly felt lost, alone and deserted. "I'm going for a walk," she said swiftly before the emotions could show on her face. "I need to think."

Lindsay loved the beach when the air hinted at winter. She wore an ancient peacoat against the bite of the cold, and with her hands in her pockets, she walked the low, slow arch of rock and sand. Above the sky was calm and unrelentingly blue. The surf was wild. There was more than the scent of the sea, there was the taste of it. Here the wind blew free, and she felt it would clear her mind.

She had never considered that her mother would make a permanent move away from Cliffside. *She wasn't sure how she felt about it.* A gull swooped low over her head, and Lindsay stopped to watch it wing its way over the rocks. Three years, she thought. Three years of being wrapped up in a routine. She wasn't certain that she could function without it. Bending over, she picked up a smooth, flat stone. It was sand-colored, speckled with black, the size of a silver dollar. Lindsay brushed it clean, then dropped it into her pocket. She kept her hand over it, absently warming it as she walked.

She thought over each stage of her life since her return to Cliffside. Casting her mind back, she recalled her years in New York. Two different lives, Lindsay mused, hunching her shoulders. Perhaps I'm two different people. As she tossed back her head, she saw the Cliff House. It was high above her and still perhaps a quarter of a mile off, but it warmed her as she warmed the stone.

Because it's always there, she decided, because you can depend on it. When everything else goes haywire, it stays constant. Its windows shimmered in the sun as she watched. Puffs of smoke curled, just as they should, from several chimneys. Lindsay sighed, hugging herself.

From far down the beach a movement caught her eye. Seth was

walking toward her. He must have come down the beach steps from the house. Shielding her eyes with her hands, she watched him. She was smiling before she was aware of it. *Why does he do this to me?* she wondered with a shake of her head. *Why am I always so terribly glad to see him? He walks with such confidence. No wasted motion, no superfluous movement. I'd like to dance with him, something slow, something dreamy.* She felt the tug and sighed. *I should run before he gets any closer.*

She did. Toward him.

Seth watched her coming. Her hair lifted and streamed behind her. The wind pinched pink into her cheeks. Her body seemed weightless, skimming over the sand, and he was reminded of the evening he had come upon her dancing alone. He wasn't aware that he had stopped walking.

When she reached him, her smile was brilliant. She held out her hands in greeting. "Hi." Rising on her toes, she brushed his mouth with a quick kiss. "I'm so glad to see you. I was lonely." Her fingers laced with his.

"I saw you from the house."

"Did you?" She thought he looked younger with his hair ruffled by the wind. "How did you know it was me?"

There was the faintest of frowns in his eyes, but his voice was untroubled. "The way you move."

"No greater compliment for a dancer. Is that why you came down?" It felt good to feel his hands again, to see the solemn, studying look in his eyes. "To be with me?"

Only his eyebrow moved—in a slight upward tilt—before he answered. "Yes."

"I'm glad." She smiled warmly, without reservation. "I need someone to talk to. Will you listen?"

"All right."

In silent agreement, they began to walk.

"Dancing has always been in my life," Lindsay began. "I can't remember a day without classes, a morning without the barre. It was vital to my mother, who had certain limitations as a dancer, that I go further. It was very fortunate for everyone that I wanted to dance and that I could. It was important to us in different ways, but it was still a bond."

Her voice was quiet but clear against the roar of the sea. "I was only a bit older than Ruth when I joined the company. It's a hard life; the competition, the hours, the pressure. Oh God, the pressure. It begins in the morning, the moment your eyes open. The barre, classes, rehearsals, more classes. Seven days a week. It's your life; there's nothing else. There can't be anything else. Even after you begin to ease your way out of the *corps,* you can't relax. There's always someone behind you, wanting your place. If you miss a class, one class, your body knows it and tortures you. There's pain—in the muscles, the tendons, the feet. It's the price necessary to maintain that unnatural flexibility."

She sighed and let the wind buffet her face. "I loved it. Every moment of it. It's difficult to understand how it feels to be standing there in the wings before your first solo. Another dancer knows. And when you dance, there isn't any pain. You forget it because you have to. Then, the next day, it starts again.

"When I was with the company, I was completely wrapped up in myself, in my work. I rarely thought of Cliffside or anyone here. We were just going into rehearsals for *Firebird* when my parents had the accident." She paused here, and though her voice thickened, it remained steady. "I loved my father. He was a simple, giving man. I doubt if I thought of him more than a dozen times that last year in

New York. Have you ever done something, or not done something, that you periodically hate yourself for? Something you can't change, ever?"

"Something that wakes you up at three o'clock in the morning?" Seth slipped an arm around Lindsay's shoulders and drew her closer to him. "A couple of times."

"My mother was in the hospital a long time." For a moment she turned her face into his shoulder. It was more difficult to speak of it than she had anticipated. "She was in a coma, and then there were operations, therapy. It was long and painful for her. There were a lot of arrangements I had to make, a lot of papers I had to go through. I found out they'd taken a second mortgage on the house to finance my first two years in New York." A deep breath helped to hold back tears. "I'd been there, totally fixated on myself, totally involved with my own ambitions, and they were putting up their home."

"It must have been what they wanted to do, Lindsay. And you succeeded. They were obviously proud of you."

"But you see, I just took it from them without any thought, without any gratitude."

"How can you be grateful for something you know nothing about?" he pointed out.

"Logic," Lindsay murmured as a gull screamed over their heads. "I wish I could be more logical. In any case," she continued, "when I came back, I opened the school to keep myself sane and to help with the finances until my mother was well enough for me to leave. At that time I had no plans for staying."

"But your plans changed." Her steps had slowed, and Seth shortened his stride to suit hers.

"The months piled up." Absently, Lindsay pushed at the hair that fluttered into her line of vision. "When my mother finally got out of the hospital, she still needed a great deal of care. Andy's mother was a lifesaver. She split her time between her shop and the house so that I could keep the school going. Then there came a point when I had to face things as they were. Too much time had gone by, and there wasn't an end yet in sight."

She walked for a moment in silence. "I stopped thinking about going back to New York. Cliffside was my home, and I had friends here. I had the school. The lives of professional dancers are very regimented. They take classes every day which is far different from teaching them. They eat a certain way, they think a certain way. I simply stopped being a professional dancer."

"But your mother wouldn't accept that."

Surprised, Lindsay stopped walking and looked up at him. "How did you know?"

He brushed the hair from her cheek. "It isn't difficult."

"Three years, Seth." She shrugged her shoulders. "She isn't being realistic. I'll be twenty-six soon; how can I go back and attempt to compete with girls Ruth's age? And if I could, why should I torture my muscles, destroy my feet and starve myself a second time? I don't even know if I'm capable. I loved it there... and I love it here." She turned to watch the surf spray high over the rocks. "Now my mother plans to move away permanently, to start fresh, and I know, to force me to make a decision. A decision I thought I'd already made."

His hands came to her shoulders, the fingers light and strong. "Do you resent her moving away where you can't take care of her anymore?"

"Oh, you're very perceptive." Lindsay leaned back against him a moment. There was comfort there. "But I want her to be happy—

106

really happy—again. I love her, not in the same uncomplicated way I loved my father, but I do love her. I'm just not sure I can be what she wants."

"If you think being what she wants will pay her back, you're wrong. Life doesn't work that neatly."

"It should." Lindsay frowned at the foaming spray. "It should."

"Don't you think it might be boring if it did?" His voice was quiet and controlled above the screams of the gulls and the roar of the waves. Lindsay was glad, very glad, she had run toward him and not away. "When is your mother leaving?"

"In three weeks."

"Then give yourself some time after she's gone to decide where your life's heading. There's too much pressure on you now."

"I should have known you'd be logical." She turned to him and was smiling again. "Usually, I resent that kind of advice, but this time it's a relief." She slipped her arms around his waist and buried her face in his chest. "Will you hold me? It feels so good to depend on someone else for just a minute."

She seemed very small when his arms came around her. Her slightness appealed to his protective instincts. Seth rested his cheek on the top of her head and watched the water war against the rocks.

"You smell of soap and leather," Lindsay finally murmured. "I like it. A thousand years from now I'll remember you smelled of soap and leather." She lifted her face and searched deep in his eyes. I could fall in love with him, she thought. He's the first man I could really fall in love with.

"I know I'm crazy," she said aloud, "but I want you to kiss me. I want so badly to taste you again."

Their mouths met slowly to linger, to savor. They drew away once, far enough to see the need mirrored in each other's eyes, then

107

they joined again, flame for flame. The taste and texture of his mouth was familiar now, but no less exciting. Lindsay clung to him. Their tongues teased only, hinting of what could be. The well of desire was deeper than she had known, and its waters more treacherous. For a moment she gave herself to him utterly. Promises trembled on her lips.

Quickly, Lindsay pushed away, shaking her head. She placed a hand to her head, smoothing her hair back from her face as she took a long breath.

"Oh, I should stay away from you," she whispered. "Very far away."

Seth reached up to cup her face in his hand. "It's too late for that now." Passion was still dark in her eyes. With only the slightest pressure, he brought her back a step.

"Maybe." She placed her hands on his chest but neither pushed away nor drew closer. "In any case, I asked for this."

"If it were summer," he said and trailed his fingers down her throat, "we'd have a picnic here, late at night with cold wine. Then we'd make love and sleep on the beach until dawn came up over the water."

Lindsay felt the tremors start at her knees. "Oh yes," she said on a sigh. "I should stay away from you." Turning, she sprinted for a clump of rocks. "Do you know why I like the beach best in early winter?" she called out as she scrambled to the top.

"No." Seth walked over to join her. "Why?"

"Because the wind is cold and alive, and the water can be mean. I like to watch it just before a storm."

"You enjoy challenges," Seth remarked, and Lindsay looked down at him. The height gave her a unique perspective. "Yes, I do. So do you, as I recall. I read that you're quite a parachutist."

He held a hand up to her, smiling as their fingers touched. Lindsay wrinkled her nose and jumped lightly to the sand. "I only go as far off the ground as I can without apparatus," she said and cocked a brow. "I'm not about to go leaping out of a plane unless it's parked at the airport."

"I thought you enjoyed a challenge."

"I also enjoy breathing."

"I could teach you," Seth offered, drawing her into his arms.

"You learn to do a *tour en l'air,* and I'll learn to jump. Besides..." Lindsay struggled from his arms as a recollection struck her. "I remember reading that you were teaching some Italian countess to free fall."

"I'm beginning to think you read entirely too much." Seth grabbed her hand and pulled her back.

"I'm surprised you've had time to build anything with such an active social life."

His grin was a quick, youthful flash. "I'm a firm believer in recreation."

"Hmm." Before Lindsay could mull over an answer, a flash of red caught her eye from a short distance down on the beach. "It's Ruth," she said, twisting her head.

Ruth raised her hand once hesitantly as she crossed the sand toward them. Her hair hung loose over a scarlet jacket. "She's a lovely girl." Lindsay turned to face Seth again. She saw as he, too, watched Ruth, but there was a frown in his eyes. "Seth?" He looked down at her. "What is it?" she asked with concern.

"I might have to go away for a few weeks. I worry about her; she's still so fragile."

"You don't give her enough credit." Lindsay tried to ignore the sudden sense of loss his words gave her. *Go away?* Where? When? She focused on Ruth and forced the questions away. "Or yourself," she added. "You've built a relationship. A few weeks won't damage it or Ruth."

Before he could answer, Ruth had joined them.

"Hello, Ms. Dunne." Her smile had become more relaxed since the first time Lindsay had seen it. There was a welcome sparkle of excitement in her eyes. "Uncle Seth, I've just come from Monica's. Her cat had kittens last month."

Lindsay laughed. "Honoria is single-handedly responsible for the feline population explosion in Cliffside."

"Not single-handedly," Seth commented dryly, and Lindsay laughed again.

"She had four," Ruth continued. "And one of them…well…" She glanced from Seth to Lindsay, catching her bottom lip between her teeth. Silently, she pulled open the snaps of her jacket and revealed a tiny bundle of orange fur.

Lindsay let out an inevitable squeal as she reached out and took the velvety kitten from Ruth. She buried her nose in its fur. "He's beautiful. What's his name?"

"Nijinsky," Ruth told her and turned her dark eyes to her uncle. "I'd keep him upstairs in my room where he wouldn't be in Worth's way. He's little and won't be any trouble," she rushed on hopefully.

Lindsay looked up as Ruth spoke. Animation had lit her eyes. In Lindsay's experience with her, only dancing had brought that much life to her face. "Trouble?" she said, automatically allying herself with the girl. "Of course he won't be any trouble. Just look at that face." She pushed the kitten into Seth's hands. Seth took a finger and tilted the kitten's face upward. Nijinsky mewed and settled down to sleep again.

"Three against one," Seth said as he scratched the furry ears. "Some might consider that foul play." He gave the kitten back to Ruth, then ran a hand down her hair. "Better let me handle Worth."

"Oh, Uncle Seth." Cradling the kitten, Ruth tossed her free arm around Seth's neck. "Thank you! Ms. Dunne, isn't he wonderful?"

"Who?" Her eyes danced above Ruth's head. "Nijinsky or Seth?"

Ruth giggled. It was the first time Lindsay had heard the uniquely girlish sound from her. "Both of them. I'm going to take him in." She snapped the small bundle back inside her jacket and began to jog across the sand. "I'll sneak some milk from the kitchen," she called back behind her.

"Such a small thing," Lindsay murmured, watching the bright red jacket disappear down the stretch of sand. She turned to Seth with a nod of approval. "You did that very well. She thinks she persuaded you."

Seth smiled and caught at Lindsay's wind-tossed hair. "Didn't she?"

Lindsay returned his smile and gave in to the urge to touch his cheek. "I like knowing you're a soft touch." She dropped her hand. "I have to go."

"Lindsay." He held her still when she tried to turn away. "Have dinner with me." The look in his eyes was intimate. "Just dinner. I want you with me."

"Seth, I think we both know we wouldn't just have dinner. We'd both want more."

"Then we'll both have more," he murmured, but when he drew Lindsay into his arms, she resisted.

"No, I need to think." For a moment she rested her forehead against his chest. "I don't think clearly when you're touching me. I need some time."

"How much?" He put his hand under her chin to lift her face.

"I don't know." The tears that sprang to her eyes stunned them both. Astonished, Lindsay brushed at them. Seth lifted a finger and trapped one on the tip.

"Lindsay." His voice was gentle.

"No, no, don't be kind. Yell at me. I'll get control of myself if you yell at me." She put both hands to her face and took deep breaths. Quite suddenly, she knew what had brought on the tears. "I have to go. Please let me go, Seth. I need to be alone."

From the pressure of his hands, she was afraid he would refuse. "All right," he said after a long moment. "But I'm not known for my patience, Lindsay."

She didn't respond but turned and fled. Fleeing with her was the realization not only that she could fall in love with Seth Bannion, but that she already had.

Chapter 9

They drove to the airport in the early afternoon. Andy drove with Lindsay beside him and both their mothers in the back seat. The trunk was cramped with luggage. Even after the three weeks of helping her mother prepare for the move, a cloud of disbelief hung over Lindsay. Already, boxes had been shipped ahead to California, and the house she had grown up in was on the market.

When it was sold, she knew her last ties to her childhood would go with it. It's for the best, she thought as she listened to her mother and Carol chatter in the rear seat. Everything I need will fit into the spare room at the school. It'll be more convenient for me, and there isn't any doubt that it's best for Mother.

She watched a plane gliding toward the ground and knew they were almost there. Her thoughts seemed to drift with the aircraft. Since the day Mae had announced her plans, Lindsay hadn't functioned at top level. Too many emotions had surfaced that day. She had tried to lock them away until she could deal with them rationally, but they had been too powerful. Again and again, they had escaped to haunt her dreams, or worse, to catch her unprepared in the middle of a class or conversation. She hadn't wanted

113

to think about Seth, but she had: once when Monica had innocently brought up his name, again when Ruth had smuggled the kitten into class and dozens of other times when something reminded her of him.

It was odd how she could no longer walk into a room where he had been without associating it with him. Even her own studio reminded her of Seth.

After the initial shock had settled, Lindsay had explored the adventure of being in love. It didn't make her light-headed, as some songs promised, but it did make her less attentive to ordinary things. She hadn't lost her taste for food, but sleep had become a problem. She wasn't walking on clouds, but found herself, instead, waiting for the storm to hit. It was not falling in love that dictated her reactions, she decided, but the person with whom she had chosen to fall in love.

Chosen, Lindsay repeated silently, paying no attention as Andy worked his way through airport traffic. If I could have chosen who I'd fall in love with, it would've been someone who adored me, someone who thought I was perfection and whose life would be totally devoted to making mine Utopia.

Oh, no you wouldn't have, she corrected. Her window reflected the ghost of her smile. That would've bored me to death in a week. Seth suits me entirely too well. He's totally in command of himself, very cool, yet sensitive. Trouble is, he's a man who's made a career out of avoiding commitments...except for Ruth. She sighed and touched her own reflection with a fingertip. And there's another problem. It's difficult to be so totally opposed to something that's so important to both of us. How can we get closer when we're on opposite sides of a sixty-foot fence?

It was Andy's voice that brought Lindsay's mind back to present company. Disoriented, she glanced about to see that they had parked and that the others were already climbing out of the car. Quickly, Lindsay got out and tried to catch up with the conversation.

"...since we've already got our tickets and a car waiting at LAX," Carol finished as she pulled a suitcase and tote bag from the trunk.

"You will have to check all this baggage," Andy reminded her, easily hefting three more cases with a garment bag slung over his shoulder. "Catch the trunk, will you, Lindsay?" he asked absently as she was left with only her own purse and a cosmetic case.

"Sure."

Carol winked at Mae as Lindsay slammed the trunk shut and pulled out the keys. The wind billowed the hem of her coat. Glancing up, she scanned the sky. "It'll be snowing by nightfall."

"And you'll be trying on new bathing suits," Lindsay grumbled obligingly as she tried to move the two women along. The air was sharp and stung her cheeks.

Inside the terminal, there was the usual last-minute confusion about locating tickets and securing boarding passes. After checking the luggage, Andy began a detailed verbal listing of the do's and don'ts his mother was to follow.

"Keep the baggage checks in your wallet."

"Yes, Andy."

Lindsay caught the gleam in Carol's eye, but Andy continued to frown.

"And don't forget to call when you get to L.A."

"No, Andy."

"You have to set your watch back three hours."

"I will, Andy."

"And don't talk to strange men."

Carol hesitated. "Define strange," she demanded.

"Mom." His frown turned up into a grin before he enveloped her in a crushing hug.

Lindsay turned to her mother. She wanted it over quickly, without strain. But when they faced each other, her glib parting speech became lost. She was a child again, with words running riot in her mind. Instead of trying to sort through them, she threw her arms around her mother's neck.

"I love you," she whispered, shutting her eyes tight on tears. "Be happy. Please, please, be happy."

"Lindsay." Her name was a softly spoken sigh. After a moment, Mae drew away. They were of the same height, and their eyes were level. It was strange, but Lindsay couldn't remember the last time her mother had looked at her with such total concentration. Not at the dancer, but at her daughter.

"I love you, Lindsay. I might've made mistakes," Mae sighed with the admission. "But I always wanted the best for you—what I thought was the best. I want you to know I'm proud of you."

Lindsay's eyes widened, but her throat closed on any response. Mae kissed both her cheeks, then, taking the case from her hands, turned to say goodbye to Andy.

"I'm going to miss you," Carol said on a quick, energetic hug. "Go after that man," she whispered in Lindsay's ear. "Life's too short." Before Lindsay could answer, she, too, had kissed her. She walked with Mae through the gate.

When they were gone, Lindsay turned to Andy. Tears dampened her lashes, but she managed to prevent them from rolling down her cheeks. "Should I feel like an orphan?"

He smiled and slipped an arm around her. "I don't know, but I do. Want some coffee?"

Lindsay sniffled, then shook her head. "Ice cream," she said positively. "A great big ice cream sundae because we should be celebrating for them." She linked her arm with his as they began to walk away from the gate. "I'm treating."

Carol's weather forecast was right on the mark. An hour before sunset, the snow began. It was announced by Lindsay's evening students as they arrived for class. For several moments she and her students stood in the cold of the opened doorway and watched it fall.

There was always something magical about the first snow, Lindsay thought. It was like a promise, a gift. By midwinter, snow would bring grumbling and complaints, but now, fresh and soft and white, it brought dreams.

Lindsay continued the class, but her mind refused to settle. She thought of her mother landing in Los Angeles. It would still be afternoon there, and sunny. She thought of the children here in Cliffside who would be dragging their sleds out of attics and storerooms and sheds in preparation for tomorrow's rides. She thought of taking a long, solitary walk on the snowy beach. She thought of Seth.

It was during the break between classes, when her students were changing shoes for *pointe* class, that Lindsay went to the door again. The wind had picked up, and it tossed snow into her face. There were six inches or more on the ground already, and it was falling thickly. At that rate, Lindsay calculated, there would be well over a foot before the class was finished. Too risky, she decided, and shut the door.

"No *pointe* class tonight, ladies." Rubbing her arms to restore circulation, she moved back into the room. "Who has to call home?"

It was fortunate that the majority of Lindsay's advanced students drove or car pooled to class. Arrangements were soon made for the younger ones to be dispatched, and after the obligatory confusion, the studio was cleared. Lindsay took a deep breath before turning to Monica and Ruth.

"Thanks. That exodus would've taken twice the time if you hadn't helped." She looked directly at Ruth. "Have you called Seth?"

"Yes. I'd already made plans to stay at Monica's tonight, but I checked in."

"Good." Lindsay sat down and began to pull a pair of corduroy slacks over her tights and leg warmers. "I'm afraid this is going to turn into a solid blizzard in another hour or so. I want to be home with a cup of hot chocolate by then."

"I like the sound of that." Monica zipped up a down-filled parka, then pulled on the hood.

"You look ready for anything," Lindsay commented. She was carefully packing toe and ballet shoes into a tote bag. "What about you?" she asked Ruth as she pulled a ski cap down over her ears. "Ready?"

Ruth nodded and joined the women as they walked to the door. "Do you think classes will be on schedule tomorrow, Ms. Dunne?"

Lindsay opened the door, and the three of them were buffeted by the wind. Wet snow flew into their faces. "Such dedication," Monica mumbled, lowering her head to force her way across the parking lot.

By tacit agreement, all three began by clearing off Monica's car, sharing the broom Lindsay had brought with her from the studio. In short order, the car was unearthed, but before they could turn to give Lindsay's the same attention, Monica let out a long groan. She pointed to the left front tire.

"Flat," she said dully. "Andy told me it had a slow leak. He told me to keep air in it. Shoot." She kicked the offending tire.

"Well, we'll punish you later," Lindsay decided. She stuck her hands in her pockets, hoping to keep her fingers warm. "Right now, I'll take you home."

"Oh, but Lindsay!" Distress poured from Monica's eyes. "It's so far out of your way."

Lindsay thought a moment, then nodded. "You're right," she said briskly. "Guess you'll have to change that tire. See you tomorrow." Hefting the broom over her shoulder, she started toward her car.

"Lindsay!" Monica grabbed Ruth's hand, and the two ran after the departing figure. Along the way, Monica scooped up a fistful of snow and laughingly tossed it at Lindsay's ski cap. Her aim was flawless.

Lindsay turned, unconcerned. "Want a lift?" The expression on Ruth's face had her bubbling with laughter. "Poor thing, she thought I meant it. Come on." Generously, she handed Monica the broom. "Let's get moving before we're buried in this stuff."

In less than five minutes Ruth was sandwiched between Lindsay and Monica in the front seat. Snow swirled outside the windshield and danced in the stream of the headlights. "Here goes," Lindsay said and took a deep breath as she put the car in first.

"We were in a snowstorm once in Germany." Ruth tried to make herself smaller to avoid cramping Lindsay as she drove. "We had to travel on horseback, and when we reached the village, we were snowbound for three days. We slept on the floor around a fire."

"Got any other bedtime stories?" Monica asked. She closed her eyes against the rapidly falling snow.

"There was an avalanche," Ruth supplied.

"Terrific."

"We haven't had one of those here in years," Lindsay stated as she crept cautiously along.

"I wonder when the snow plows will be out." Monica frowned at the street, then at Lindsay.

"They've already been out; it's just hard to tell. They'll be busy

119

tonight." Lindsay shifted, keeping her eyes on the road. "See if that heater's warmed up yet. My feet are freezing."

Obediently, Ruth switched it on. There was a blast of cold air. "I don't think it's ready," she hazarded, switching it off again. Out of the corner of her eye, Lindsay caught the smile.

"You're just smug because you've battled avalanches."

"I did have on pile-lined boots," Ruth admitted.

Monica wriggled her toes inside her thin loafers. "She's a smart aleck," she said conversationally. "The reason she gets away with it is because she does it with such innocence. Look." She pointed upward and to the right. "You can just see the lights of the Cliff House through the snow."

The urge was irresistible; Lindsay glanced up. The faint brightness of artificial light shone through the curtain of snow. She felt almost as though she were being pulled toward it. The car skidded in response to her inattention. Monica shut her eyes again, but Ruth chattered away, unconcerned.

"Uncle Seth's working on drawings for a project in New Zealand. It's beautiful, even though it's only pictures. You can tell it's going to be fabulous."

Cautiously, Lindsay turned the corner toward Monica's house. "I suppose he's pretty busy these days."

"He closes himself up in his office for hours," Ruth agreed. She leaned forward to try the heater again. This time the air was tepid. "Don't you love winter?" she asked brightly. Monica moaned, and Lindsay burst out laughing. "She is a smart aleck," she agreed. "I might not have noticed if you hadn't pointed it out."

"I didn't detect it myself all at once," Monica told her. She was beginning to breathe a bit easier as they made their way slowly down the block toward her house. When they pulled up in her driveway,

Monica heaved a sigh of relief. "Thank goodness!" She shifted in her seat, crushing Ruth as she leaned toward Lindsay. Ruth found she liked the companionable discomfort. "Stay here tonight, Lindsay. The roads are awful."

Lindsay shrugged off the concern. "They're not that bad yet." The heater was humming along nicely now, and she felt warm and confident. "I'll be home in fifteen minutes."

"Lindsay, I'll worry and bite my nails."

"Good grief, I can't be responsible for that. I'll call you the minute I get home."

"Lindsay…"

"Even before I fix the hot chocolate."

Monica sighed, recognizing defeat. "The very minute," she ordered sternly.

"I won't even wipe my feet on the way to the phone."

"Okay." She climbed out of the car and stood amidst the thickly falling snow as Ruth followed. "Be careful."

"I will. Good night, Ruth."

"Good night, Lindsay." Ruth bit her lip at the slip in propriety, but Monica was already closing the door. No one else had noticed. Ruth smiled as she watched Lindsay's headlights recede.

Lindsay backed slowly out of the driveway and headed up the road. She switched on the radio to fill the void left by Monica and Ruth. The roads, as Monica had said, were awful. Though her wipers were working at top speed, they afforded her only scant seconds of vision before the windshield was covered again. It took every bit of her concentration and skill to keep the car from sliding. She was a good driver and knew the roads intimately, yet there was a small knot of tension at the base of her neck. Lindsay didn't mind it. Some people work best under pressure, and she considered herself one of them.

She pondered a moment on why she had refused Monica's invitation. Her own house would be dark and quiet and empty. The refusal had been automatic, and now she found herself regretting it. She didn't want to brood or to be alone. She was tired of thinking.

For a moment she vacillated between going ahead and going back. Before she could reach a firm decision, a large, black shape darted into the road ahead of her. Lindsay's brain barely had enough time to register that the shape was a dog before she was whipping the wheel to avoid a collision.

Once the skid had begun, she had no control. As the car spun, spitting up snow from the wheels, she lost all sense of direction. There was only the blur of white. Firmly, she controlled panic and resisted the urge to slam on the brakes. The fear that bubbled in her throat had no time to surface. It happened fast. The car struck something hard, and there was no slow-motion interlude before it slammed to a halt. She felt a flash of pain and heard the music on the radio turn to static before there was only the silence and the dark....

Lindsay moaned and shifted. There was a fife and drum corps marching inside her head. Slowly, because she knew she'd have to eventually, she opened her eyes.

Shapes floated and dimmed, then swam into focus. Seth frowned down at her. She felt his fingers on the side of her head where the pain was concentrated. Lindsay swallowed because her throat felt dry, but her voice was still husky when she spoke.

"What are you doing here?"

He raised a brow. She watched the change in the slant of its tip. Without speaking, he lifted her lids one at a time and studied her pupils carefully.

"I had no idea you were a complete idiot." The words were calmly spoken. In her dazed state, Lindsay didn't detect the edge of temper. She started to sit up, only to have him place his hand on her shoulders to hold her down. For the moment, she lay back without protest. She was, she discovered, on the sofa in his parlor. There was a fire in the hearth; she could hear its crackle and smell the hint of wood smoke. Its flames cast shadows into a room lit only by two muted china lamps. There was a needleworked pillow under her head, and her coat was still buttoned. Lindsay concentrated on each trivial fact and sensation until her mind began to come to order.

"That dog," she said, abruptly remembering. "Did I hit that dog?"

"What dog?" Impatience was evident in Seth's voice, but she plunged on.

"The dog that jumped out in front of the car. I think I missed him, but I can't be sure...."

"Do you mean to tell me that you ran into a tree to avoid hitting a dog?" If Lindsay had possessed all her faculties, she would have recognized the danger of the icy calm. Instead, she reached up gingerly to finger the ache at her temple.

"Is that what I hit? It feels more like I ran into an entire forest."

"Lie still," he ordered, leaving Lindsay staring as he strode from the room.

Cautiously, she persuaded her body into a sitting position. Her vision remained clear, but her temple throbbed abominably. Leaning her head back against the cushions, she closed her eyes. As a dancer, she was used to pain and to coping with it. Questions began to form in her mind. Lindsay let them shape and dissolve and regroup until Seth came back into the room.

"I thought I told you to lie still."

Lindsay opened her eyes and gave him a wan smile. "I'll do better sitting up, really." She accepted the glass and pills he thrust at her. "What are these?"

"Aspirin," he muttered. "Take them." Her brow lifted at the command, but the ache in her head persuaded her to give in gracefully. Seth watched her swallow before he walked across the room to pour brandy. "Why the hell didn't you stay at Monica's?"

Lindsay shrugged, then leaned back against the cushion again. "I was asking myself that same question when the dog jumped into the road."

"And you hit the brakes in a snowstorm to avoid running into him." The disgust was ripe in his tone. Lindsay opened one eye to stare at his back, then closed it again.

"No, I turned the wheel, but I suppose it amounts to the same thing. I didn't think, though I imagine I'd have done the same thing if I had. In any case, I don't think I hit him, and I'm not damaged much, so there's little harm done."

"Little harm done?" Seth paused in the act of handing her a brandy. The tone of his words caused both of her eyes to open. "Do you have any idea what might have happened to you if Ruth hadn't called and told me you'd driven her to Monica's?"

"Seth, I'm not really very clear on what happened other than that I lost control of my car and hit a tree. I think you'd better clear up the basic facts before we argue."

"Drink some of this." He gave her the brandy snifter. "You're still pale." He waited until she obeyed, then went back to pour his own. "Ruth phoned to let me know she was safe at Monica's. She told me you'd driven them, then insisted on driving yourself home."

"I didn't insist, exactly," Lindsay began, then, noting Seth's expression, she shrugged and sampled the brandy again. It wasn't the hot chocolate she had envisioned, but it was warming.

"Monica was quite naturally worried. She said you'd be driving past shortly and asked, since I've such a good view of the road, if I'd keep a lookout for you. We assumed there wouldn't be much traffic in this miserable weather." He paused to drink, then swirled the remaining brandy while he looked at her. Faint color was returning to her cheeks. "After I hung up, I went to the window, just in time, it seems, to see your headlights. I watched them veer, then circle, then stop dead." After setting the brandy down, he thrust his hands into his pockets. "If it hadn't been for that phone call, you could very well still be in that car unconscious. Thank God you at least had enough sense to wear your seat belt, otherwise you'd have a great deal more than a bump on your head."

She bristled defensively. "Listen, I hardly intended to knock myself unconscious, and I..."

"But you did," Seth inserted. His tone was quiet and clipped.

"Seth, I'm trying very hard to be grateful, as I assume it was you who got me out of the car and up to the house." She drank the rest of her brandy, then set down the snifter. "You're making it difficult."

"I'm not interested in your gratitude."

"Fine, I won't waste it, then." Lindsay rose. The movement was too swift. She had to dig her nails into her palms to drive away the dizziness. "I'd like to call Monica so she won't be worried."

"I've already called." Seth watched the color the brandy had restored drain. "I told her you were here, that you had car trouble. It didn't seem necessary to tell her what kind. Sit down, Lindsay."

"That was very sensible of you," she returned. "Perhaps I could impose further on you to drive me back to Monica's."

Seth walked to her, placed his hands on her shoulders, and meeting her angry eyes, shoved her back down on the sofa. "Not a chance. Neither one of us is going back out in that storm."

Lindsay lifted her chin and aimed a glare. "I don't want to stay here."

"At this point, I don't think you have much choice," he retorted.

Lindsay shifted, crossing her arms over her chest. "I suppose you'll have Worth make up a room in the dungeon."

"I might," he agreed. "But he's in New York seeing to some business for me." He smiled. "We're quite alone."

Lindsay tried to make an unconcerned gesture with her shoulders, but the movement came off as a nervous jerk. "It doesn't matter; I can walk to Monica's in the morning. I suppose I could use Ruth's room."

"I suppose."

She rose, but more slowly than the first time. The throbbing was down to a dull ache, easily ignored. "I'll go up, then."

"It's barely nine." The hand on her shoulder was light but enough to stop her. "Are you tired?"

"No, I..." The truth was out before she thought to prevaricate.

"Take off your coat." Without waiting for her response, he began undoing the buttons himself. "I was too preoccupied with trying to bring you around to worry about it before." As he slipped the coat from her shoulders, his eyes came back to hers. Gently, he touched a finger to the bruise on her temple. "Hurt?"

"Not much now." Lindsay's pulse rate had quickened. There was no use trying to blame it on the shock of the accident. Instead, she admitted to the feelings that were beginning to swim inside her and met his eyes directly. "Thank you."

He smiled as he ran his hands up her arms, then back down to her fingers.

A moan escaped when he lifted both of her hands to kiss the insides of her wrists. "Your pulse is skittish."

"I wonder why," she murmured. Pleased, Seth gave a low laugh as he released her hands.

"Have you eaten?"

"Eaten?" Lindsay's mind tried to focus on the word, but her senses were still dominating her system.

"Food," Seth supplied. "As in dinner."

"Oh, no, I've been at the studio since this afternoon."

"Sit down, then," he ordered. "I'll go see if Worth left anything palatable."

"I'll come with you." She placed her hand on his to halt his objection. "Seth, we dancers are a sturdy breed. I'm fine."

He studied her face critically, then nodded. "All right, but my way." In an unexpected move, he swept her up in his arms. "Humor me," he said, anticipating her objection.

Lindsay found the sensation of being pampered delicious and settled back to enjoy it. "Have you eaten?"

Seth shook his head. "I've been working.... Then I was distracted."

"I've already thanked you," Lindsay pointed out. "I won't apologize on top of it. It was the dog's fault anyway."

Seth nudged open the kitchen door with his shoulder. "It wouldn't be an issue if you'd done the sensible thing and stayed at Monica's."

"There you go, being logical again." Lindsay heaved a sigh as he set her down at the kitchen table. "It's a nasty habit, but I'm certain you could break it." She smiled up at him. "And if I'd stayed at Monica's, I wouldn't be here right now being waited on. What are you going to fix me?"

Seth captured her chin in his hand and examined her closely. "I've never known anyone like you."

His voice was brooding, so she touched his hand with hers. "Is that good or bad?"

He shook his head slowly, then released her. "I haven't made up my mind."

Lindsay watched him walk to the refrigerator. It was hard for her to believe how much she loved him—how complete and solid the love had already become.

And what do I do about it? she asked herself. Do I tell him? How embarrassing that would be for him, and how completely I would ruin what seems to be the beginning of a great friendship. Isn't love supposed to be unselfish and understanding? Spreading her fingers on the table's surface, she stared at them. But is it supposed to hurt one minute and make you feel like flying the next?

"Lindsay?"

She looked up sharply, suddenly aware that Seth had spoken to her. "I'm sorry." She smiled. "I was daydreaming."

"There's a platter of roast beef, a spinach salad and a variety of cheeses."

"Sounds terrific." Lindsay stood, holding up a hand to quiet his protest. "I'm off the critical list, I promise. I'll trust you to put all that together while I set the table." She walked to a cupboard and began searching.

"How do you feel about washing dishes?" Lindsay asked while Seth made after-dinner coffee.

"I've given the subject very little thought." He glanced back over his shoulder. "How do you feel about it?"

Lindsay leaned back in her chair. "I've just been in an accident. Very traumatic. I doubt whether I'm capable of manual labor just yet."

"Can you walk into the other room?" he asked dryly. He lifted a tray. "Or shall I take the coffee in and come back for you?"

"I'll try." Lindsay pushed herself away from the table. She held open the door and allowed Seth to pass through.

"Actually, most people wouldn't bounce back as quickly as you have." They moved down the hall together. "You took a pretty good whack, from the size of the bump on your head. And from the look of your car, you're lucky it wasn't more."

"But it wasn't," Lindsay pointed out as they came to the parlor. "And please, I don't want to know about my car until I have to. That could send me into severe depression." Sitting on the sofa, she gestured for Seth to set the tray on the table in front of her. "I'll pour. You take cream, don't you?"

"Mmm." Seth moved over to toss another log on the fire. Sparks shot out before the log hissed and caught. When he came back to her, Lindsay was pouring her own cup. "Are you warm enough?"

"Oh yes, the fire's wonderful." She sat back without touching her coffee. "This room's warm even without it." Snug and relaxed, she allowed her eyes to wander and appreciate. "When I was a teenager, I used to dream about sitting here just like this…a storm outside, a fire in the grate and my lover beside me."

The words tumbled out without thought. The moment they had, Lindsay's cheeks went wild with color. Seth touched the back of his hand to her face.

"A blush is something I didn't expect to see on you." Lindsay caught the hint of pleasure in his voice. She shifted away.

"Maybe I'm feverish."

"Let me see." Seth turned her back to face him. Firmly, he held her still, but the mouth that lowered to her brow was gentle as a whisper. "You don't seem to be." One hand trailed up to the pulse at her throat. His fingers pressed lightly. "Your pulse isn't steady."

"Seth…" She let his name trail off into silence as he slid a hand under her sweater to caress her back. He ran a fingertip along the path where the leotard gave way to flesh.

"But perhaps you're too warm with this heavy sweater."

"No, I. . ." Before she could prevent him, he had expertly slipped it over her head. Her skin was rosy warm beneath.

"That's better." He kneaded her bare shoulders briefly, then turned back to his coffee. Every nerve in Lindsay's body had been awakened. "What else did you dream about?" As he drank, his eyes sought hers. Lindsay wondered if her thoughts were as transparent as she feared.

"About dancing with Nicky Davidov."

"A realized dream," Seth commented. "Do you know what fascinates me about you?"

Intrigued, Lindsay shook her head. At her stern orders, her nerves began to settle. "My stunning beauty?" she suggested.

"Your feet."

"My feet!" She laughed on the words, automatically glancing down at the canvas slip-ons she wore.

"They're very small." Before Lindsay had any notion of his intent, he had shifted her feet into his lap. "They should belong to a child rather than a dancer."

"But I'm lucky enough to be able to support them on three toes. A lot of dancers can only use one or two. Seth!" She laughed again as he slipped her shoes off.

The laughter stilled as he trailed a finger down her instep. Incredibly, she felt a fierce rush of desire. It poured into her, then spread like wildfire through her system. Her quiet moan was involuntary and irrepressible.

"They appear very fragile," Seth commented, cupping her arch in his palm. "But they must be strong." Again he lifted his eyes to hers.

His thumb trailed over the ball of her foot, and she shuddered. "And sensitive." When he lifted her feet and kissed both of her ankles, Lindsay knew she was lost.

"You know what you do to me, don't you?" she whispered. It was time to accept what had to be between them.

There was a gleam of triumph in his eyes as he lifted his head again. "I know that I want you. And that you want me."

If it were only that simple, Lindsay thought. If I didn't love him, we could share each other with total freedom, without regrets. But I do love him, and one day I'll have to pay for tonight. There was a light flutter of fear in her chest at the thought of what the price might be.

"Hold me." She went into his arms and clung. "Hold me." While the snow lasts, she told herself, we're alone. There's no one else in the world, and this is our time. There's no tomorrow. There's no yesterday.

She tilted back her head until she could see his face. With a fingertip, she slowly traced the curves and angles until she knew every inch was carved in her memory.

"Love me, Seth," she said with her eyes wide. "Make love with me."

There was no time for a gentleness neither of them wanted. Passion sets its own rules. His mouth was avid, burning on hers before her words had dissolved in the air. His hunger was unbearably arousing. But she sensed he was in control, still the captain of their destiny. There was no fumbling as he undressed her. His hands caressed her as each layer of clothing was removed, inciting desire wherever they touched. When she struggled to release the buttons of his shirt, he helped her. There was fire and need and spiraling pleasure.

Touching him, exploring the taut flesh of his chest and shoulders,

Lindsay felt yet a new sensation. It was one of possession. For now, for the moment, he belonged to her, and he owned her absolutely. And they were flesh to flesh without barriers, naked and hungry and tangled together. His mouth roamed down feverishly to taste her breast, then lingered there, savoring, while his hands brought her trembling delight. His tongue was excitingly rough. As he nuzzled, she moved under him, powered by needs that grew in velocity and strength.

Her breath came in whimpers as she urged his lips back to hers. They came on a slow journey, pausing at her throat, detouring to her ear until she was near madness for the taste of him. Ravenously, she took his mouth with hers, shuddering now with a passion more all-consuming than anything she had ever experienced. In the dance, she remained one unit. The pleasure and dreams were hers and within her control. Now, she was joined to another, and pleasure and dreams were a shared thing. The loss of control was a part of the ecstasy.

She felt strong, more powerful than it seemed possible for her to be. Her energy was boundless, drawn from the need to have, the need to give. Their passion flowed sweet as honey; she was molten in his arms.

Chapter 10

Lindsay dreamed she was lying in a big, old bed, wrapped in quilts and in her lover's arms. It was a bed that knew their bodies well, one she had awakened in morning after morning over the years. The sheets were Irish linen and soft as a kiss. The quilt was an heirloom she would pass on to her daughter. The lover was a husband whose arms became only more exciting over the years. When the baby cried, she stirred, but lazily, knowing that nothing could disturb the tranquil beauty in which she lived. She snuggled deep into the arms that held her and opened her eyes. Still dreaming, she smiled into Seth's.

"It's morning," she murmured and found his mouth warm and soft and delightful. She ran her fingertips down his spine, smiling when his lips became more insistent. "I've got to get up," she whispered, nestling as his hand cupped her breast. She could still hear the faint, plaintive cry of the baby.

"Uh-uh." His lips moved to her ear. Slowly, his tongue began to awaken her fully. Passion rekindled the night's embers.

"Seth, I have to, she's crying."

With a half-hearted oath, Seth rolled over and reached down to the floor. Rolling back, he plopped Nijinsky the cat on Lindsay's stomach. She blinked, disoriented and confused as the kitten mewed at her, making sounds like a baby. The dream shattered abruptly.

Lindsay reached up to drag a hand through her hair and took a long breath.

"What's the matter?" Seth tangled his hand in her hair until she opened her eyes.

"Nothing." She shook her head, stroking the kitten so that he purred. "I was dreaming. It was silly."

"Dreaming." He brushed his lips over her naked shoulder. "About me?"

Lindsay turned her head until their eyes met again. "Yes." Her lips curved. "About you."

Seth shifted, bringing her to rest in the curve of his shoulder. Nijinsky moved to curl at their feet. He circled twice, pawed the quilt, then settled. "What was it about?"

She burrowed into the column of his throat. "My secret." His fingers were trailing soothingly over her shoulder and upper arm.

I belong to him, she thought, *and can't tell him.* Lindsay stared at the window, seeing that though the snow was thinning, it fell still. There's only the two of us, she reminded herself. Until the snow stops, there's just we two. *I love him so desperately.* Closing her eyes, she ran her hand up his chest to his shoulder. There were muscles there she wanted to feel again. With a smile, she pressed her lips against his throat. There was today. *Only today.* She moved her mouth to his, and their lips joined.

Their kisses were short, quiet tastes. The rush—the desperation—of the night before had mellowed. Now desire built slowly, degree by degree. It smoldered, it teased, but it didn't overpower. They took time to enjoy. Seth shifted so that she lay across his chest.

"Your hands," he murmured as he brought one to his lips, "are exquisite. When you dance, they seem to have no bones." He spread his hand over hers, palm to palm.

Her hair cascaded around her shoulders to fall on his. In the soft, morning light it was as pale as an illusion. Her skin was ivory with touches of rose just under the surface. It was a fragile, delicately boned face, but the eyes were vivid and strong. Lindsay lowered her mouth and kissed him, long and lingeringly. Her heartbeat quickened as she felt his hunger build.

"I like your face." She took her mouth from his to softly kiss his cheeks and eyelids and jaw. "It's strong and just a bit wicked." She smiled against his skin, remembering. "You terrified me the first time I saw you."

"Before or after you ran out in the road?" He trailed one hand up her back while the other stroked her hair. It was a lazy, comfortable loving.

"I did not run out in the road," Lindsay nipped at his chin. "You were driving too fast." She began to plant kisses down the length of his chest. "You looked awfully tall when I was sitting in that puddle."

She heard him chuckle as he ran a hand down the arch of her back, then slowly reacquainted himself with the slight flare of her hips, the long length of her thighs.

He shifted, and they moved as one until their positions were reversed. The kiss deepened. The touch of hands to flesh was still gentle but more demanding now. Conversation lapsed into a soft slumber. Passion rose like a tropical wave, warm and steep. It crested, then receded....

Dressed in jeans and a flannel shirt borrowed from Ruth's wardrobe, Lindsay skipped down the main stairway. There was a chill in the house which told her the fires had yet to be lit. Only the one in the master bedroom crackled. The first stage of her plan was to start one in the kitchen hearth. She hummed an impromptu tune as she pushed open the door.

It surprised her that Seth was there ahead of her. She could smell the coffee.

"Hi!" Walking over, she wrapped her arms around his waist, resting her cheek on his back. "I thought you were still upstairs."

"I came down while you were using Ruth's barre." Turning, he gathered her close. "Want some breakfast?"

"Maybe," she murmured, nearly exploding with joy at the simple intimacy. "Who's going to fix it?"

He tilted her chin. "We both are."

"Oh." Her brows lifted. "I hope you like cold cereal and bananas. That's my specialty."

Seth grimaced. "Can't you do anything with an egg?"

"I make really pretty ones at Easter time."

"I'll scramble," he decided, then kissed her forehead. "Can you handle toast?"

"Possibly." With her head resting against his chest, she watched the snow fall.

The trees and lawn resembled a stage set. The white blanket on the ground lay completely unmarred. The evergreen shrubs Seth had planted were wrapped in their own snowy coats; towering above them nearby, the trees stood as snow-covered giants. And still it fell.

"Let's go outside," Lindsay said impulsively. "It looks wonderful."

"After breakfast. We'll need more wood, in any case."

"Logical, logical." Lindsay wrinkled her nose at him. "Practical, practical." She let out a quick cry when he tugged her earlobe playfully.

"Architects have to be logical and practical, otherwise buildings fall down and people get upset."

"But your buildings don't look practical," Lindsay told him. She watched him as he walked to the refrigerator. Who, exactly, was this man she was in love with? Who was the man who had laid claim to her emotions and her body? "They always look beautiful, never like those steel and glass boxes that rob cities of their character."

"Beauty can be practical, too." He turned back with a carton of eggs in one hand. "Or perhaps it's better to say practicality can be beautiful."

"Yes, but I should think it more difficult to make a really good building appealing to the eye as well as functional."

"If it isn't difficult, it's hardly worth the trouble, is it?"

Lindsay gave a slow nod. That she understood. "Will you let me see your drawings of the New Zealand project?" She wandered to the bread box. "I've never seen the conception of a building before."

"All right." He began to break eggs into a bowl.

They prepared and ate the meal in easy companionship. Lindsay thought the kitchen smelled of family; coffee and toast and singed eggs. She logged the scent in her memory file, knowing it would be precious on some future morning. When they had eaten and set the kitchen to rights, they piled on layers of outdoor clothing and left the house.

Lindsay's first step took her thigh-deep in snow. Laughing, Seth gave her a nudge that sent her sprawling backward. She was quickly up to her shoulders. The sound of his laughter hit the wall of snow and bounced back, accentuating their solitude.

"Maybe I'd better put a bell around your neck so I can find you," he called out, laughing.

Lindsay struggled to stand up. Snow clung to her hair and crusted

137

her coat. Seth's grin widened as she scowled at him. "Bully," she said with a sniff before she began to trudge through the snow.

"The wood pile's over here." Seth caught her hand. After giving token resistance, Lindsay went with him.

Their world was insular. Snow tumbled from the sky to disappear into the thick blanket around them. She could barely hear the sea. Ruth's boots came to her knees, but with every step, snow trickled inside the tops. Her face was rosy with cold, but the view outbalanced every discomfort.

The whiteness was perfect. There was no glare to sting the eyes, nor any shadows to bring variations in shade. There was simply white without relief, without obstruction.

"It's beautiful," Lindsay murmured, pausing as they reached the woodpile. She took a long, sweeping view. "But I don't think it could be painted or photographed. It would lose something in the duplication."

"It'd be flat," Seth told her. He stacked wood into her arms. Lindsay's breath puffed out in front of her as she gazed beyond his shoulder.

"Yes, that's it exactly." The agreement pleased her. "I'd rather remember it than see it in one dimension." With Seth alongside, she made slow progress to the back door. "But you must be an expert at visualizing reality from a flat drawing."

"You've got it backwards." They stacked the wood behind the utility room door. "I make drawings from a reality I visualize."

Lindsay stopped a moment, a bit breathless from the exertion of wading through thigh-deep snow. "Yes." She nodded. "I can understand that." Studying him, she smiled. "You've snow on your eyelashes."

His eyes searched hers questioningly. She tilted her head, inviting the kiss. His lips lowered to touch hers, and she heard him suck in his breath as he lifted her into his arms.

He carried her over the threshold and through the door. When he continued through the utility room into the kitchen, Lindsay roused herself to object. "Seth, we're covered with snow. It's going to drip everywhere."

"Yep."

They were in the hall, and she pushed the hair from her eyes. "Where are you going?"

"Upstairs."

"Seth, you're crazy." She bounced gently on his shoulder as he climbed the main staircase. "We're making a mess. Worth's going to be very upset."

"He's resilient," Seth stated, turning into the master bedroom. He placed Lindsay onto the bed. From her reclining position she pushed herself up onto her elbows.

"Seth." He had removed his coat and was working on his boots. Lindsay's eyes widened, half in amusement, half in disbelief. "Seth, for goodness sake, I'm covered with snow."

"Better get out of those wet things, then." He tossed his boots aside, then moved to her to unbutton her coat.

"You're mad," she decided, laughing as he drew off her coat and tossed it on the floor to join his boots.

"Very possibly," he agreed. In two quick tugs, he had removed her boots. The thick wool socks she wore were stripped off before he began to massage warmth back into her feet. He felt her instant response to his touch.

"Seth, don't be silly." But her voice was already husky. "Snow's melted all over the bed."

With a smile, he kissed the balls of her feet and watched her eyes cloud. Moving to her side, he gathered her into his arms. "The rug is dry," he said as he lowered her. Slowly, his fingers following his mouth, he undid the buttons of her shirt. Beside them, the fire he had built before breakfast sizzled.

He parted her shirt, not yet removing it. With a tender laziness he began kissing her breasts while Lindsay floated on the first stage of pleasure. She sighed once, then, touching his cheek with her hand, persuaded his mouth to hers. The kiss began slowly, but the quality changed without warning. His mouth became desperate on a groan that seemed to come from somewhere deep inside him. Then he was tugging at the rest of her clothes, impatient, tearing the seam in Ruth's shirt as he pulled it from Lindsay's shoulder.

"I want you more than before," he mumbled as his teeth and lips grew rough at her neck. "More than yesterday. More than a moment ago." His hands bruised as they took possession of her body.

"Then have me," she told him, drawing him closer, wanting him. "Have me now."

Then his mouth was on hers and there were no more words.

The phone woke Lindsay. Drowsily, she watched Seth rise to answer it. He wore the forest green robe he had slipped on when he had rebuilt the fire. She had no sense of time. Clocks were for a practical world, not for dreams.

She stretched slowly, vertebra by vertebra. If forever could be a moment, she would have chosen that one. She felt soft and warm and well-loved. Her body was heavy with pleasure.

Lindsay watched Seth without hearing the words he spoke into the phone. He stands so straight, she thought and smiled a little. And he so rarely uses gestures with his words. Gestures can betray feelings, and his are very private. He holds his own leash. *Her smile sweetened.* And I like knowing I can take him to the end of it.

His voice intruded into her musings as snatches of his conversation leaked through. *It's Ruth,* she realized, distracted from her concentrated study of his face. After sitting up, Lindsay drew the quilt around her shoulders. Before she looked to the window, she knew what she would see. The snow had stopped while they slept. She waited for Seth to hang up the phone.

She managed to smile at him while her mind worked feverishly to gather impressions; the way his hair fell over his forehead, the glint of the sun on it as light spilled through the window, the straight, attentive way he stood. Her heart seemed to expand to hold new degrees of love. She fought to keep her face composed.

Don't spoil it, she ordered herself frantically. *Don't spoil it now.* It seemed to Lindsay that Seth was studying her with even more than his usual intensity. After a long moment, he crossed to where she sat on the floor, cocooned by quilts and pillows.

"Is she coming home?" Lindsay asked when Seth replaced the receiver.

"She and Monica are driving over shortly. The county's been on the ball, it seems, and the roads are nearly clear."

"Well," Lindsay pushed at her hair before she rose, still tented by the quilt. "I suppose I'd better get ready, then. It seems I'll have evening classes."

There was a sudden outrageous desire to weep. Lindsay battled against it, bundling herself up in the quilt as she gathered her clothes. *Be practical,* she instructed. *Seth is a practical man. He'd hate emotional scenes.* She swallowed hard and felt control returning. While slipping into her tights and leotard, she continued to talk.

"It's amazing how quickly these road crews work. I can only hope

141

they didn't bury my car. I suppose I'll have to have it towed. If it's only a minor disaster, I shouldn't be without it for long." Dropping the quilt, she slipped her sweater over her head. "I'll have to borrow Ruth's brush," she continued, pulling her hair out from the collar. Suddenly, she stopped to face Seth directly. "Why do you just look at me?" she demanded. "Why don't you say something?"

He stood where he was, still watching her. "I was waiting for you to stop babbling."

Lindsay shut her eyes. She felt completely defenseless. She had, she realized, made an utter fool of herself. This was a sophisticated man, one used to casual affairs and transitory relationships. "I'm simply no good at this sort of thing," she said. "I'm not good at it at all." He reached for her. "No, don't." Quickly, she jerked away. "I don't need that now."

"Lindsay." The annoyance in his tone made it easier for her to control the tears.

"Just give me a few minutes," she snapped at him. "I hate acting like an idiot." With this, she turned and fled the room, slamming the door behind her.

In fifteen minutes Lindsay stood in the kitchen pouring Nijinsky a saucer of milk. Her fine hair was brushed to fall neatly down her back. Her nerves, if not quiet, were tethered. Her hands were steady.

The outburst had been foolish, she decided, but maybe it had helped ease her into the first stage of her return to the outside world.

For a moment she lost herself in a dream as she gazed out on the world of white. She knew, though he made no sound, the moment Seth stepped into the room. Lindsay took an extra second, then turned to him. He was dressed in dark brown corduroy slacks and a vee-neck sweater over a pale blue shirt. She thought he looked casually efficient.

"I made some coffee," she said in a carefully friendly voice. "Would you like some?"

"No." He came toward her purposefully; then, while she was still wondering what he would do, he brought her close. His hands circled her upper arms. The kiss was searing and long and enervating. When he drew her away, Lindsay's vision dimmed and then refocused.

"I wanted to see if that had changed," he told her while his eyes seemed to spear into hers. "It hasn't."

"Seth..." But his mouth silenced hers again. Protest became hungry response. Without thought, she poured every ounce of her feelings into the kiss, giving him all. She heard him murmur her name before he crushed her against him. Again, all was lost. The flashes of paradise came so swiftly, Lindsay could only grasp at them without fully taking hold. Drawn away again, she stared up at him, not seeing, only feeling.

Another woman, she thought dazedly, would be content with this. Another woman could continue to be his lover and not hurt for anything else. Another woman wouldn't need so much from him when she already has so much. Slowly, Lindsay brought herself back. The only way to survive was to pretend she was another woman.

"I'm glad we were snowbound," she told him, pulling gently from his arms. "It's been wonderful being here with you." Keeping her voice light, she walked back to the coffeepot. When she poured, she noticed her hand was no longer steady.

Seth waited for her to turn back, but she continued to face the stove. "And?" he said, slipping his hands into his pockets.

Lindsay lifted the coffee cup and sipped. It was scalding. She smiled when she turned. "And?" she repeated. The hurt was thudding inside her throat, making the word painful.

His expression seemed very much as it had the first time she had seen him. Stormy and forbidding. "Is that all?" he demanded.

Lindsay moistened her lips and shrugged. She clung to the cup with both hands. "I don't think I know what you mean."

"There's something in your eyes," he muttered, crossing to her. "But it keeps slipping away. You won't let me know what you're feeling. Why?"

Lindsay stared into the cup, then drank again. "Seth," she began calmly and met his eyes again. "My feelings are my business until I give them to you."

"Perhaps I thought you had."

The hurt was unbelievable. Her knees trembled from it. His eyes were so steady, so penetrating. Lindsay took her defense in briskness. "We're both adults. We were attracted to each other, we have been for some time...."

"And if I want more?"

His question scattered her thoughts. She tried to draw them back, tried to see past the guard that was now in his eyes. Hope and fear waged war inside her. "More?" she repeated cautiously. Her heart was racing now. "What do you mean?"

He studied her. "I'm not certain it's an issue if I have to explain it."

Frustrated, Lindsay slammed her cup back on the counter. "Why do you start something and not finish it?"

"Exactly what I'm asking myself." He seemed to hesitate, then lifted a hand to her hair. She leaned toward him, waiting for a word. "Lindsay..."

The kitchen door swung open in front of Ruth and Monica.

144

"Hi!" Ruth's greeting trailed off the moment she took in the situation. She searched quickly for a way to back out, but Monica was already passing her to go to Lindsay.

"Are you okay? We saw your car." Concern dominated her tone as she reached out to touch her friend. "I knew I should've made you stay."

"I'm fine." She gave Monica a kiss for reassurance. "How're the roads now?"

"Pretty good." She jerked her head at Ruth. "She's worried about missing class."

"Naturally." Lindsay gave her attention to the girls until her pulse leveled. "That shouldn't be a problem."

Attracted by Ruth's voice, Nijinsky wandered over to circle her legs until she obliged him by picking him up. "Are you sure you feel up to it?"

Lindsay read the knowledge in Ruth's eyes and reached for her cup again. "Yes. Yes, I'm fine." Automatically she went to the sink for a cloth to wipe up the coffee she had spilled. "I guess I should call a tow truck."

"I'll see to it." Seth spoke for the first time since the interruption. His tone was formal and distant.

"That isn't necessary," Lindsay began.

"I said I'll see to it. I'll take you all to the studio when you're ready." He walked from the room, leaving the three of them staring at the swinging door.

Chapter 11

Monica and Ruth rode in the back of Seth's car on the drive to the studio. Ruth was conscious of a definite, pronounced tension between her uncle and Lindsay. Whatever was between them, she concluded, had hit a snag. Because she was fond of both of them, Ruth did her best to ease the strained atmosphere. "Is Worth due back tonight?"

Seth met her eyes briefly in the rearview mirror. "In the morning."

"I'll fix you coq au vin tonight," she volunteered, leaning forward onto the front seat. "It's one of my best dishes. But we'll have to eat late."

"You have school tomorrow."

"Uncle Seth." Her smile was tolerant. "I'm graduating from high school, not elementary school.

"Monica showed me her brother's yearbook last night," she continued, turning her attention to Lindsay. "The one from the year you and Andy graduated."

"Andy looked great in his football jersey, didn't he?" Lindsay shifted in her seat so that she faced Ruth.

"I liked your picture best." She pushed her hair back over her shoulder. Lindsay saw that all her shyness had fled. Her eyes were as open and friendly as her smile. "You should see it, Uncle Seth. She's on the steps leading into the auditorium. She's doing an *arabesque*."

"Smart aleck Tom Finley told me to do a little ballet."

"Is that why you were sticking out your tongue?"

Lindsay laughed. "It added to the aesthetic value of the photograph."

"It sounds like a good likeness," Seth commented, turning both Lindsay's and Ruth's attention to himself. "The *arabesque* was in perfect form, I imagine. You could dance in the middle of an earthquake."

Lindsay kept her eyes on his profile, not certain if he was praising her or criticizing her. "It's called concentration, I suppose."

"No." Seth took his eyes from the road long enough to meet her gaze. "It's called love. You love to dance. It shows."

"I don't think there's a better compliment," Ruth said. "I hope someone says that to me one day."

All the things she wanted to say raced through Lindsay's mind, but none would remain constant. Instead, she laid her hand on the back of his. Seth glanced at their hands, then at Lindsay. "Thank you," she said.

Her heart caught when he turned his hand over to grip hers. He brought it to his lips. "You're welcome."

Ruth smiled at the gesture, then settled back as they turned into the school parking lot. Someone had made a halfhearted attempt to clear the snow, and Lindsay knew immediately that it must have been the neighborhood kids.

"Someone's here," Ruth commented when she spotted the sleek foreign car parked in the lot.

Lindsay absently glanced away from Seth as he stopped the car. "I wonder who..." The words stumbled to a halt, and her eyes widened. She shook her head, certain she was wrong, but climbed slowly out of the car. The man in the black overcoat and fur hat stepped away from the studio door and walked to her. The moment he moved, Lindsay knew she wasn't mistaken.

"Nikolai!" Even as she shouted his name, she was racing through the snow. She saw only a blur of his face as she flung herself into his arms. Memories poured over her.

He had held her before; the prince to her Giselle, the Don to her Dulcinea, Romeo to her Juliet. She had loved him to the fullest extent of friendship, hated him with the pure passion of one artist for another, worshipped his talent and despaired of his temper. As he held her again, everything they had shared, everything she had felt in her years with the company, flooded back to her. The wave was too quick and too high. Weeping, she clung to him.

Nick laughed, pulling her away to give her a boisterous kiss. He was too absorbed with Lindsay to hear Ruth's reverently whispered *"Davidov"* or to see Seth's concentrated study.

"Hello, *ptichka,* my little bird." His voice was high and rich with Russian inflection. Lindsay could only shake her head and bury her face in his shoulder.

The meeting was unexpected, whipping up her already heightened emotions. But when he drew her away again, she saw through her blurred vision that he was precisely the same. Though he had a deceptively innocent boy's face, he could tell ribald jokes and swear in five languages. His thickly lashed blue eyes crinkled effectively at the corners. His mouth was generous, romantically shaped, and there was the charm of two slight dimples when he smiled. His hair was dark blond, curling and thick. He left it tousled to his advan-

148

tage. He skimmed under six feet, making him a good partner for a dancer of Lindsay's size.

"Oh, Nick, you haven't changed." Lindsay touched his face with both hands. "I'm so, so glad you haven't."

"But you, *ptichka,* you have changed." The potent choirboy grin lit his face. "You are still my little bird, my *ptichka,* but how is it you are still more beautiful?"

"Nick." Tears mixed with laughter. "How I've missed you." She kissed his cheeks, then his mouth. Her eyes, washed with tears, were shades deeper. "What are you doing here?"

"You weren't home, so I came here." He shrugged at the simplicity. "I told you I'd come in January. I came early."

"You drove from New York in all this snow?"

Nikolai took a deep breath and looked around. "It felt like Russia, your Connecticut. I like to smell the snow." His eyes alit on Seth and Ruth. "Your manners are revolting, *ptichka,*" he said mildly.

"Oh, I'm sorry! I was so surprised...." She felt flustered and brushed at her tears with the back of her hand. "Seth, Ruth, this is Nikolai Davidov. Nicky, Seth and Ruth Bannion. She's the dancer I told you about."

Ruth stared at Lindsay. In that moment, she became Lindsay's willing slave.

"A pleasure to meet friends of Lindsay's." He shook hands with Seth. A small line appeared between his brows as he studied him. "You are not perhaps the architect Bannion?"

Seth nodded while Lindsay watched the men measure each other. "Yes."

Nick beamed with pleasure. "Ah, but I have just bought a house of your design in California. It's on the beach with many windows so that the sea is in the living room."

He's so effusive, Lindsay thought of Nick. So different from Seth, and yet they remind me of each other.

"I remember the house," Seth acknowledged. "In Malibu?"

"Yes, yes, Malibu!" Obviously delighted, Nick beamed again. "I'm told it's early Bannion, reverently, as though you were long dead."

Seth smiled as people invariably did with Nick. "The more reverently, the higher the market value."

Nikolai laughed offhandedly, but he had caught the expression in Lindsay's eyes when she looked at Seth. So, he thought, that's the way the wind blows. "And this is the dancer you want to send me." He turned his attention to Ruth, taking both hands in his. He saw a small, dark beauty—with good bones and narrow hands—who trembled like a leaf. The face would be exotic with the right makeup and lighting, he decided. And her size was good.

"Mr. Davidov." Ruth struggled not to stutter. To her, Nikolai Davidov was a legend, a figure larger than life. To be standing toe to toe with him, her hands held by his, seemed impossible. The pleasure was excruciating.

He chafed her hands, and his smile was personal. "You must tell me if Lindsay's manners are always so appalling. How long does she usually keep her friends standing out in the cold?"

"Oh, blast!" Lindsay fumbled for her keys. "You completely stun me by popping up from nowhere, then expect me to behave rationally." She pushed open the front door. "I was right," she told him over her shoulder, "you haven't changed."

Nikolai wandered past her into the room's center without speaking. Pulling off his gloves, he tapped them idly against his palm as he surveyed the studio. Ruth hung on his every movement.

"Very good," he decided. "You've done well here, *ptichka*. You have good students?"

"Yes." Lindsay smiled at Ruth. "I have good students."

"Have you found a teacher to run your school when you come back to New York?"

"Nick." Lindsay paused in the act of unbuttoning her coat. "I haven't agreed to come back."

"That is nonsense." He dismissed her objection with a flick of the wrist. It was a gesture Lindsay remembered well. An argument now would be heated and furious. "I must be back in two days. I direct *The Nutcracker*. In January I begin staging for my ballet." As he spoke, he shrugged out of his coat. He wore a simple gray jogging suit and looked, to Ruth's mind, magnificent. "With you as my Ariel, I have no doubt as to its success."

"Nick…"

"But I want to see you dance first," he said over her protest, "to make certain you haven't gone to pot."

"Gone to pot?" Incensed, Lindsay tossed her coat over a chair. "You'll be writing Russian phrase books long before I go to pot, Davidov."

"That's yet to be seen." He turned to Seth as he slipped off his hat. "Tell me, Mr. Bannion, do you know my *ptichka* well?"

Seth turned his eyes to Lindsay, holding them there until she flushed. "Fairly well." His gaze slid back to Nikolai. "Why?"

"I wonder if you could tell me if she has kept her muscles as well-exercised as her temper. It's important that I know how much time I must spend whipping her back into shape."

"Whipping me back into shape!" Knowing she was being maneuvered didn't prevent Lindsay from falling into the trap. "I don't need you or anyone to whip me into shape."

"Okay." He nodded as he looked down at her feet. "You need toe shoes and tights, then."

Lindsay turned on her heel and headed for her office. Still fuming, she slammed the door behind her. Nick grinned at Seth and Ruth.

"You know her very well," Seth commented.

Nikolai gave a quick chuckle. "As I know myself. We are very much the same." Reaching into a deep pocket of his coat, he produced a pair of ballet shoes. He sat on a chair to change into them. "You've known Lindsay long?" Nikolai knew he was prying and realized from the lift of Seth's brow that the bluntness had been acknowledged.

He is a private, self-contained man, Nikolai decided. But his thoughts are on Lindsay. If it was a man who was keeping her from resuming her profession, he wanted to know it and to understand the man. He concluded that Seth wouldn't be an easy man to understand. Complications, he knew, appealed to Lindsay.

"A few months," Seth answered at length. The artist in him recognized an extraordinarily beautiful man. The sensitive face held just enough puckishness to keep it from being too smooth. It was a face easily cast as a fairy-tale prince. A difficult face to dislike. Seth slipped his hands into his pockets. He, too, felt a desire to understand the man.

"You worked together for some time in New York."

"I've had no better partner in my career," he said simply. "But I could never say so to my *ptichka*. She works best when her passions are aroused. She has great passions." He smiled as he rose. "Like a Russian."

Lindsay came back into the room wearing black tights and a leotard with white leg warmers and *pointe shoes*. Her chin was still lifted.

"You've put on some weight," Nikolai commented as he gave her willow slim figure a critical survey.

152

"I'm a hundred and two," she said defensively.

"You'll need to drop five pounds," he told her as he walked to the barre. "I'm a dancer, not a weight-lifter." He *pliéd* while Lindsay caught her breath in fury.

"I don't have to starve myself for you anymore, Nick."

"You forget, I'm director now." He smiled at her blandly and continued to warm up.

"You forget," she countered, "I'm not with the company now."

"Paperwork only." He gestured for her to join him.

"We'll leave you two alone." Lindsay turned to Seth as he spoke. Nikolai watched the contact of their eyes. *This man gives nothing away,* he decided. "And give you some privacy."

"Please," Nikolai interrupted Lindsay's response. "You must stay."

"Yes, Nick never could perform without an audience." She smiled, reaching out to touch Seth's hand. "Don't go."

"Please, Uncle Seth." Enraptured by the possibility of watching her two favorite artists perform impromptu, Ruth clung to Seth's arm. Her eyes were dark with excitement.

Seth hesitated. He looked once at Lindsay, long and deep. "All right."

The formality was back in his tone and troubled her. Why, she thought as she walked to join Nikolai, was the closeness between them so elusive? She spoke to Nick casually as they loosened and warmed their muscles, but he noted how often her eyes drifted to Seth's reflection in the glass.

"How long have you loved him?" he murmured in a voice only Lindsay could hear. She glanced up sharply. "You could never hold a secret from me, *ptichka.* A friend often sees more clearly than a lover."

"I don't know." Lindsay sighed, feeling the weight of it settle on her. "Sometimes it feels like forever."

"And your eyes are tragic." He stopped her from turning away by placing a hand to her cheek. "Is love so tragic, my little bird?"

Lindsay shook her head, trying to dispel the mood. "What sort of question is that from a Russian? Love is meant to be tragic, isn't it?"

"This isn't Chekhov, *ptichka*." After patting her cheek, he walked to the CD player. "Perhaps Shakespeare would suit you." He glanced up from the CDs he sifted through. "Do you remember the second *pas de deux* from *Romeo and Juliet?*"

Lindsay's eyes softened. "Of course I do. We rehearsed endlessly. You pulled my toes when they cramped, then threw a sweaty towel at me when I missed a *sauté.*"

"Your memory is good." He inserted the CD and programmed the selection. "Come then, dance with me now, *ptichka,* for old times and for new." Nikolai held out his hand. There was magic when they came together.

Their fingers touched, then parted. Lindsay felt it instantly: the youth, the hope, the poignancy of first love. Her steps were instinctive. They flowed with the music and paired fluidly with Nick's. When he lifted her the first time, she felt as though she was lost forever in the music, in the emotion.

Ruth watched them, hardly daring to breathe. Although the dance looked deceptively simple, her training gave her a complete appreciation of its intricacies and difficulties. It was romance in its purest form: a man and a woman irresistibly drawn together, testing the waters of new love. The music vibrated with the emotion of a love deep and doomed. It shone naked in Lindsay's eyes when she looked at Davidov. Here was not the teasing sauciness of her Dulcinea, but the vulnerabilities of a girl loving for the first time. And when they knelt on the floor, fingertips reaching for fingertips, Ruth's heart nearly burst from the glory of it.

For several seconds after the music ended, the dancers remained still, eyes locked, fingers just touching. Then Davidov smiled, and moving close, pulled her to him. She trembled lightly under his palm.

"It seems you haven't gone to pot after all, *ptichka*. Come back with me. I need you."

"Oh, Nick." Drained, she laid her head on his shoulder. She had forgotten the depth of the pleasure that was hers when she danced with him. And yet, the very essence of the dance had intensified her feelings for Seth.

If she could have gone back to the snowbound house, cut off from all in the world but him, she would have done so blindly. Her mind seemed almost drugged with wants and doubts. She clung to Nick as if he were an anchor.

"She was not too bad." Over Lindsay's head, he grinned at Seth and Ruth.

"She was wonderful," Ruth responded in a voice husky with feeling. "You were both wonderful. Weren't they, Uncle Seth?"

Slowly, Lindsay lifted her head. When she looked up at him, her eyes were still brimming with love. "Yes."

Seth watched her, but there was no expression on his face. "I've never seen two people move together more perfectly." He stood, lifting his coat as he did so. "I have to go." He laid his hand on Ruth's shoulder as he heard her murmur of disappointment. "Perhaps Ruth could stay. There's only an hour or so before her class."

"Yes, of course." Lindsay stood, uncertain how to deal with the distance that was suddenly between them. Her body still quivered with emotions that belonged to him. "Seth…" She said his name, knowing nothing else.

"I'll pick her up tonight." He shifted his attention to Nikolai, who had risen to stand beside Lindsay. "A pleasure meeting you, Mr. Davidov."

"And for me," Nikolai responded. He could feel the vibrations of distress from Lindsay as Seth turned away.

She took a step, then stopped herself. The night had been her dream, the dance her fantasy. She closed her eyes tight as the door shut behind him.

"Lindsay." Nick touched her shoulder, but she shook her head furiously.

"No, please. I—I have to make some phone calls." Turning, she fled into her office.

Nick sighed as the door clicked shut. "We are an emotional lot, dancers," he commented as he turned to Ruth. Her eyes were dark and wide and young. "Come, then, you will show me why Lindsay would send you to me."

Stunned, Ruth stared at him. "You want—you want me to dance for you?" Her limbs turned to lead. Never would she be able to lift them.

Nick nodded briskly, suddenly all business. "Yes." His eyes drifted to the closed door as he moved back to the CD player. "We will give Lindsay the time she needs for her phone calls, but we need not waste it. Change your shoes."

Chapter 12

Ruth couldn't believe what was happening. As she hurried to exchange boots for ballet shoes, her fingers seemed numbed and unable to function. *Davidov* wanted to see her dance. It was a dream, she was certain. The fantasy was so long-standing and far-fetched that she was positive she would wake up at any moment in her high, soft bed at the Cliff House.

But she was sitting in Lindsay's studio. To reassure herself, Ruth put her mind to work fiercely, checking and rechecking all points of reference while her hands tugged at the boots. There was the long, inescapable wall of mirrors; the shining, always spotless wood floor. She looked at the familiar sheet music piled on the piano, the CDs scattered on the stand. The struggling plant Lindsay had nursed so carefully sat in front of the east window. Ruth could see that another leaf had wilted. She could hear the click and hum of the heater, which had been switched on. The fan whirred softly.

Not a dream, she told herself. This was real. Her trembling hand slipped the favored ballet shoes onto her feet. She rose, daring at last to look at Davidov.

He should have been undistinguished in the plain gray jogging suit, but he wasn't. Ruth, despite her youth, recognized that certain men could never be ordinary. Some drew notice without effort. It was more than his face and physique, it was his aura.

When he had danced with Lindsay, Ruth had been transported. He was no teenage Romeo but twenty-eight, perhaps at the zenith of his career as a dancer. But she had believed him because he had exuded tender youth and the wonder of first love. No one would question any role Nick Davidov chose to portray. Now she tried to see the man but was almost afraid to look. The legend was very important to her. She was still young enough to want indestructible heroes.

She found him remarkably beautiful, but the demand of his eyes and the slight crookedness of his nose prevented it from being too smooth a face. Ruth was glad without knowing why. Now she could see only his profile as he poured over Lindsay's collection of CDs. There was a faint gleam of perspiration on his forehead testifying to the exertion of the dance he had just completed. His eyebrows were lowered, and though he studied the CD insert in his hand, Ruth wondered if his mind was on it. He seemed distant, in a world of his own. She thought perhaps that was how legends should be: remote and unapproachable.

Yet Lindsay had never been, she reflected. And Davidov had not seemed so at first. He had been friendly, she remembered. He had smiled at her.

Perhaps he's forgotten about me, she thought, feeling small and foolish. Why should he want to see me dance? Her spine straightened with a surge of pride. He asked, she reminded herself. He *ordered,* was more accurate. And he's going to remember me when I'm finished, she determined as she walked to the barre to warm up. And one day, she thought, taking first position, I'll dance with him. Just as Lindsay did.

Without speaking, Davidov set down the CD he was holding and began to pace the studio. His movements were those of a caged animal. Ruth lost her timing in simple awe. She'd been wrong; he hadn't forgotten about her, but his thoughts were focused on the woman behind the office door. He hated the look of hurt and desolation he had seen in Lindsay's eyes as she had rushed from the room.

What a range of emotions her face had held in one short afternoon, Nick mused. He'd watched Lindsay and enjoyed her surprised joy when she had seen him outside for the first time. Her eyes had brimmed with feeling. Being an emotional man, Davidov understood emotional people. He admired Lindsay's abilities to speak without words and to speak passionately.

There had been no mistaking Lindsay's feelings for Seth Bannion. He had seen it instantly. And though Seth was a controlled man, Nikolai had felt something there, too—a slight current, like a soft breath in the air. But Seth had left Lindsay without an embrace or a touch and barely a word. Nikolai felt he would never understand restrained Americans and their hesitancy to touch each other.

Still, he knew the cool departure would have hurt Lindsay. But it wouldn't have devastated her. She was too strong for that. There was something more, he was certain, something deeper. His impulses urged him to walk through the office door and demand to know the problem, but he knew Lindsay needed time. So he would give it to her.

And there was the girl.

He turned to watch Ruth warming up at the barre. The sun, slanting through the windows, flashed in the mirrors. It glowed around Ruth as she brought her leg up to an almost impossible ninety-degree angle. She held it there poised, effortlessly.

159

Nikolai frowned, narrowing his eyes. When he had looked at her outside, he had seen a lovely girl with exotic features and good bones. But he had seen a child, not yet out of the schoolroom; now he saw a beautiful woman. A trick of the light, he thought, taking a step closer. Something stirred inside him which he quickly suppressed.

Ruth moved, and the angle of the sun altered. She was a young girl again. The tension in Nick's shoulders evaporated. He shook his head, smiling at his own imagination. Sternly professional again, he walked over and selected a CD.

"Come," he said commandingly. "Take the room's center. I'll call the combination."

Ruth swallowed, trying to pretend it was every day that she danced in front of Nikolai Davidov. But she found that even taking a step from the barre was impossible. Nikolai smiled, suddenly recognizing the girl's nervousness.

"Come," he said again with more gentleness. "I rarely break the legs of my dancers."

He was rewarded by a quick, fleeting smile before Ruth walked to the center of the studio. Programming the CD selection, he began.

Lindsay had been right. Nikolai saw that within moments, but the pace of his instructions remained smooth and steady. Had Ruth been able to study him, she might have thought him displeased. His mouth was sternly set, and his eyes held an unfathomable, closed look. Those who knew him or had worked with him would have recognized unswerving concentration.

Ruth's initial terror had passed. She was dancing, and she let the music take her. An *arabesque,* a *soubresaut,* a quick, light series of *pirouettes.* She gave what he demanded her to give without question.

160

When the instructions stopped, so did she, but only to wait. She knew there would be more. She sensed it.

Nick moved back to the CD player without a glance or a word for Ruth. He sifted quickly through the CDs until he found what he wanted. "*The Nutcracker.* Lindsay does it for Christmas?" It was more of a statement than a question, but Ruth answered it.

"Yes." Her voice came strong and smooth with no more trembling nerves. She was the dancer now, the woman in control.

"You're Carla," he said with such casual confidence that Ruth thought Lindsay must have told him she had been cast in the role. He gave the combination quickly. "Show me," he demanded and folded his arms.

Inside her office, Lindsay sat silently at her desk. Nikolai's instructions to Ruth came clearly enough through the closed door, but they didn't register. She was astonished by the depth of the pain. And it kept coming—wave after wave of it. She had been so certain that she could cope with the end of her idyll with Seth, just as she had coped with the snow. She hadn't realized how much hurt there would be.

The hideous battle with tears had almost passed. She could feel the outrageous need to shed them lessen. She had sworn when she had given herself to Seth that she would never regret it and never weep. She was comforted by the knowledge that there would be memories when the pain subsided—sweet, precious memories. She had been right, she was convinced, not to have thrown herself into his arms confessing her love as she had longed to do. It would have been unbearable for both of them. She had made it easy on him by giving a casual tone to their time together. But she hadn't expected the coldness or the ease with which he had walked out of her

161

studio—and her life. She had thought for a moment, standing in his kitchen and again in the car driving to the studio, that perhaps she had been wrong after all. Imagination, Lindsay told herself with a quick shake of her head. Wishful thinking.

What had been between them had been wonderful: now it was over. That's what she had said to Seth, that's what she would have to remember.

She straightened, trying desperately to act with the same dispassion she had seen in Seth's eyes as he had turned to leave the studio. But her hands tightened into fists as emotions rose again to clog her throat. Will I stop loving him? she wondered despairingly. Can I?

Her eyes drifted to the phone, and she uncurled her hand and touched the receiver. She longed to phone him, just to hear his voice. If she could just hear him say her name. There must be a dozen excuses she could manufacture.

Idiot! She scolded herself and squeezed her eyes tightly shut. He's hardly had time to drive across town, and already you're prepared to make a fool of yourself.

It will get easier, she told herself firmly. It has to.

Rising, Lindsay moved to the window. Ice had formed along the edges of the pane. Behind the school was a high, sloping hill that curved into a narrow field. Already more than a dozen children were sledding madly. They were much too far away for her to hear the screams and laughter that must have echoed in the clear air. But she could sense the excitement, the freedom. There were trees here and there, mantled as they should be, heavy with snow and glistening in the strong sunlight.

Lindsay watched for a long time. A blur of red flew down the hill, then slowly made the trudge back to the summit. A flash of green followed to overturn halfway down and tumble to the bottom.

For a moment Lindsay wanted almost desperately to run out and join them. She wanted to feel the cold, the sharp bite of snow as it hurled into her face, the breath-stealing surge of speed. She wanted the long, aching trudge back to the top. She felt too warm—too isolated—behind the window glass.

Life goes on, she mused, leaning her brow against the cool glass. And since it won't stop for me, I'd better keep up with the flow. There isn't any backing away from it, no hiding from it. I have to meet it head on. Then she heard the evocative music of *The Nut-cracker*.

And this is where I begin.

Lindsay went to her office door, opened it and walked into the studio.

Neither Nikolai nor Ruth noticed her, and not wanting to disturb them, Lindsay came no farther into the room but stood watching Ruth who, smiling a dreamy half-smile, moved effortlessly and grace-fully to Nikolai's command. Nick watched without comment.

No one, Lindsay decided, could tell by looking at him just what was going on in his head.

It was part of his character to be as open as the wind one moment, as mysterious as the sphinx the next. Perhaps that was why he at-tracted women, she thought. Suddenly it occurred to her that he was not so very different from Seth. But it was not what she wanted to ponder at the moment, and she turned back to watch Ruth.

How young she was! Hardly more than a child despite her wise and tragic eyes. For her there should be high school proms, football games and soft summer nights. Why should the life of a seventeen-year-old be so complicated?

Lindsay pressed her fingers to her temple, trying to remember herself at the same age. She'd already been in New York, and life had been simple but very, very demanding, both for the same reason. Ballet. It was going to be the same for Ruth.

Lindsay continued to watch her dance. For some, she decided, life is not meant to be easy. She thought of herself as much as Ruth. For some it's meant to be hard, but the rewards can be so, so sweet. Lindsay remembered the incredible exhilaration of dancing on stage, the culmination of hours of work and rehearsals, the payment for all the pain and all the sacrifice. Ruth would have it as well. She was destined to. Lindsay shunned the knowledge that in order to secure what she felt was Ruth's right, she herself would have to face Seth. And in facing him, she would have to be very strong. There would be time enough to think of that in the nights ahead when she was alone. She was certain that in a few days she could cope, that she would be able to deal with her own emotions. Then she would speak to Seth about Ruth.

When the music ended, Ruth held the final position for several seconds. As she lowered her arms, the next movement began, but Nick didn't speak to her. He gave no instruction, no comment, but went instead to switch off the CD player.

Ruth, her breath coming quickly, moistened her lips. Now that the dance was finished and she could relax her concentration, every other part of her tensed. Her fingers, which had been superbly graceful during the dance, now began to tremble.

He thinks I was dreadful, and he'll tell me so, she agonized. He'll feel sorry for me and say something pacifying and kind. Both alternatives were equally horrifying to her. A dozen questions came to her mind. She wished for the courage to voice them but could only grip one hand with the other. It seemed to her that her very life was hanging in the balance, waiting for one man's opinion, one man's words.

Davidov looked over suddenly and locked eyes with her. The intensity of his gaze frightened her, and she gripped her hands together more tightly. Then the mask was gone, and he smiled at her. Ruth's heart stopped.

Here they come, she thought dizzily. Those kind, terrible words.

"Mr. Davidov," she began, wanting to stop him before he could begin. She would prefer a quick, clean cut.

"Lindsay was right," he interrupted her. "When you come to New York, come to me."

"To you?" Ruth repeated stupidly, not certain she had heard him correctly, not daring to believe.

"Yes, yes, to me." Nikolai appeared amused by Ruth's response. "I know a few things about ballet."

"Oh, Mr. Davidov, I didn't mean..." She came to him then, propelled by horrified distress. "I was just...I only meant..."

Nikolai took her hands to quiet her disjointed explanation. "How large your eyes are when you're confused," he said, giving her hands a quick squeeze. "There's still much I haven't seen, of course." He dropped her hands to take her chin and begin a thorough impassive study of her face. "How you dance on *pointe*," he continued. "How you dance with a partner. But what I've seen is good."

She was speechless. Good from Davidov was the highest of accolades.

Lindsay moved forward then, and Nikolai looked up from his study of Ruth's face. *"Ptichka?"* Releasing the girl's chin, he went to Lindsay.

Her eyes were composed and dry without any trace of red, but her face was pale. Her hand was not lifeless in his; the fingers interlocked, but they were cold. He placed his other hand over them as if to warm them.

"So, you're pleased with my prize student." There was the slightest of signals, a glimpse in her eyes there, then gone, that said what had happened was not now to be discussed.

"Did you doubt I would be?" he countered.

"No." She smiled, turning her face to Ruth. "But I'm sure she did." Lindsay looked back at Nick, and the smile was wry. "You're every bit as intimidating as your reputation, Nikolai Davidov."

"Nonsense." He shrugged off Lindsay's opinion and shot Ruth a grin. "I'm as even-tempered as a saint."

"How sweetly you lie," Lindsay said mildly. "As always."

To this he merely grinned at her and kissed her hand. "It's part of my charm."

His comfort and his friendship were easing the pain. Lindsay pressed his hand to her cheek in gratitude. "I'm glad you're here." Then, releasing his hand, she walked to Ruth. "You could use some tea," she suggested but restrained herself from touching the girl's shoulder. She wasn't yet certain the gesture would be welcomed. "Because if memory serves me, your insides are shaking right now. Mine were the first time I danced in front of him, and he wasn't nearly the legend he is now."

"I've always been a legend, *ptichka,*" Nikolai corrected. "Ruth is merely better schooled in the art of respect than you were. This one," he told Ruth with a jerk of the thumb at Lindsay, "likes to argue."

"Especially with the mighty," Lindsay agreed.

Ruth laughed a breathy, relieved, wondering sound. Could all this really be happening? she wondered. Am I actually standing here with Dunne and Davidov being treated as a professional? Looking into Lindsay's eyes, Ruth saw understanding and the faintest hint of sadness.

Uncle Seth, she remembered abruptly, ashamed of her own self-absorption. She recalled how crushed Lindsay had looked when Seth had closed the studio door behind him. Tentatively, she reached out and touched her mentor's hand.

"Yes, please, I would like some tea now."

"Russian tea?" Nikolai demanded from across the room.

Lindsay gave him a guileless smile. "Rose hips."

He made a face. "Perhaps vodka, then?" His brow rose in mild question.

"I wasn't expecting any Russian celebrities," Lindsay apologized with a smile. "There's a possibility I could dig up a diet soda."

"Tea is fine." He was studying her again, and Lindsay knew his thoughts had drifted. "Later I'll take you out for dinner, and we'll talk." He paused when Lindsay eyed him suspiciously. "Like old times, *ptichka,*" he told her innocently. "We have much to catch up on, don't we?"

"Yes," Lindsay agreed cautiously, "we do." She started to go back into her office to make the tea, but Ruth stopped her.

"I'll do it," she volunteered, recognizing that they could speak more openly without her standing between them. "I know where everything is." She darted quickly away before Lindsay could assent or decline.

Casually Nikolai slipped a CD at random from its case and inserted it into the player. The quiet romance of Chopin was enough to help insure a more private conversation. "A lovely girl," he said. "I congratulate you on your judgment."

Lindsay smiled, glancing at the door that Ruth had left partly ajar. "She'll work harder than ever now after what you said to her. You'll take her into the company, Nick," she began, suddenly eager, wanting to seal Ruth's happiness. "She..."

167

"That isn't a decision to be made in the snap of a finger," he interrupted. "Nor is it only mine to make."

"Oh, I know, I know," she said impatiently, then grabbed both of his hands. "Don't be logical, Nick, tell me what you feel, what your heart tells you."

"My heart tells me you should come back to New York." He held her fingers tighter as she started to withdraw them from his. "My heart tells me you're hurt and confused and still one of the most exquisite dancers I've ever partnered."

"We were talking about Ruth."

"You were talking about Ruth," he countered. *"Ptichka."* The quiet sound of his voice brought her eyes back to his. "I need you," he said simply.

"Oh, don't." Lindsay shook her head and closed her eyes. "That's not fighting fair."

"Fair, Lindsay?" He gave her a quick shake. "Right or wrong isn't always fair. Come, look at me." She obeyed, letting his direct, blue eyes look deep into hers. "This architect," he began.

"No," Lindsay said quickly. "Not now, not yet."

She looked pale and vulnerable again, and he lifted a hand to her cheek. "All right. Then I'll ask you this: Do you think I would want you back in the company, dancing the most important role of my first ballet, if I had any doubts about your talent?" She started to speak, but a lift of his brow halted her. "Before you talk of sentiment and friendship, think."

Taking a deep breath, Lindsay turned away from him and walked to the barre. She knew Nikolai Davidov and understood his utter selfishness when dancing was involved. He could be generous, giving, charmingly selfless personally. When it suited him. But when the dance was involved, he was a strict professional. Ballet held the lion's share of his heart. She rubbed the back of her neck, now tense again. It all seemed too much to think about, too much to cope with.

"I don't know," she murmured. Nothing seemed as clear or as certain as it had only hours before. Turning back to Nick, Lindsay lifted both hands, palms up. "I just don't know."

When he came to her, she lifted her face. He could see that hurt was still mixed with confusion. The shrill whistle of the teakettle in her office momentarily drowned out Chopin. "Later we'll talk more," he decided and slipped an arm around her. "Now we'll relax before your classes begin."

They walked across the room to join Ruth in Lindsay's office. Stopping, she gave him a quick kiss. "I am glad you're here."

"Good." He gave her a hug in return. "Then after class you can buy me dinner."

Chapter 13

On the day after Christmas, snow lay in drifts on the side of the road. Thick icicles glinted from eaves of houses while multitudes of tiny ones clung to tree branches. The air was crisp and cold, the sunlight thin.

Restless and more than a little bored, Monica walked to the town park. The playground looked abandoned and pitiful. Brushing the snow off a wooden swing, she sat down. She kicked at the snow with her boots and set herself in motion. She was worried about Lindsay.

There had been a change, a change of some magnitude. It had started right after the first snow of the season. She was not sure whether it had been brought about by the time Lindsay had spent with Seth or the visit from Nick Davidov. Moodiness was simply not a characteristic trait of Lindsay's. But time had passed, and the moodiness remained. Monica wondered if she was more sensitive to Lindsay's mood because her own was so uncertain.

Monica had been shocked to realize that the long-standing crush she had on Andy had developed into full-blown love. She had hero-worshipped him from the first day he had come home with her brother wearing his high school football jersey. She had been ten to his fifteen. Ironically, the major obstacle in her path was the person she felt closest to: Lindsay.

Why couldn't Lindsay see how crazy Andy was about her? Monica leaned far back in the swing, enjoying the flutter in her stomach as the sky tilted with her movements. It was pale blue. Why hadn't he told her? Monica pushed harder.

During the years of Lindsay's absence from Cliffside, Monica had been a love-struck teenager whom Andy had treated kindly with absent pats on the head. Since Lindsay's return, he hadn't appeared to notice that his friend's little sister had grown up. No more, Monica thought grouchily, than Lindsay had noticed Andy's heart on his sleeve.

"Hi!"

Turning her head, Monica got a quick glimpse of Andy's grin before she flew forward. On the backswing, it was still there. She dragged her feet on the ground and slowed. "Hi," she managed as he settled in her line of vision.

"You're up early for a Saturday," he commented, idly running his hand down the chain of the swing. "How was your Christmas?"

"Fine—good." She cursed herself and tried to speak coherently. "You're up early, too."

Andy shrugged, then sat on the swing beside her. Monica's heart trembled. "Wanted a walk," he murmured. "Still giving piano lessons?"

Monica nodded. "I heard you were expanding the flower shop."

"Yeah, I'm adding a whole section of house plants."

Monica studied the hands on the chains of the swing beside her. It was amazing that such large and masculine hands could arrange flowers with incredible delicacy. They were gentle hands. "Aren't you opening today?"

171

"This afternoon, for a while, I thought." He shrugged his broad shoulders. "Doesn't look like anybody's up but you and me." He turned his head to smile at her. Monica's heart cartwheeled.

"I—I like getting up early," she mumbled.

"Me, too." Her eyes were soft and vulnerable as a puppy's.

Monica's palms were hot in the December air. She rose to wander restlessly around the playground.

"Do you ever think about moving away from Cliffside?" she asked after a short silence.

"Sure." Andy pushed off the swing to walk with her. "Especially when I'm down. But I don't really want to leave."

She looked up at him. "I don't, either." Her foot kicked an abandoned ball half-buried in the snow. Stooping, Monica picked it up. Andy watched the thin winter sunlight comb through her hair. "I remember when you and my brother used to practice in the backyard." She tossed the small ball lightly. "Sometimes you'd throw me one."

"You were pretty good, for a girl," Andy acknowledged and earned a scowl. He laughed, feeling lighter than he had when he started on his walk. Monica always made him feel good. As she tossed the ball up again, he grabbed it. "Want to go out for one?"

"Okay." She jogged across the snow, then ran laterally, remembering the moves from years before. Andy drew back, and the ball sailed toward her in a sweeping arch. Perfectly positioned, she caught the ball handily.

"Not bad," Andy yelled. "But you'll never score."

Monica tucked the ball under her arm. "Watch me," she yelled back and raced through the trampled snow.

She ran straight for him, then veered off to the left before he could make the touch. Her agility surprised him, but his reflexes were good. He turned, following her zigzagging pattern. Caught up in the chase, he threw himself out, nipping her by the waist and bringing her down. They hit the snow with a muffled thud. Instantly horrified, Andy rolled her over. Her face was pink under a coating of snow.

"Oh, wow, Monica, I'm sorry! Are you okay?" He began to brush the snow from her cheeks. "I wasn't thinking. Did I hurt you?"

She shook her head but hadn't yet recovered the breath to speak. He lay half across her, busily brushing the snow from her face and hair. Their breath puffed out and merged. She smiled at his expression of horrified concern, and their eyes met. Suddenly Andy gave way to impulse and placed a light, hesitant kiss on her lips.

"Sure you're okay?" His taste was much sweeter than Monica had imagined. She tasted it again when he lowered his mouth a second time.

"Oh, Andy!" Monica threw her arms around his neck and rolled until he was positioned beneath her. Her lips descended to his, but there was nothing light or hesitant about her kiss. Snow slipped down Andy's collar, but he ignored it as his hand went to the back of her head to prolong the unexpected. "I love you," she said as her mouth roamed his face. "I love you so much."

He stroked her hair. Monica felt weightless. He seemed determined to lie there forever as Monica, soft and scented, clung to his neck. Then he sat up, still cuddling her, and looked down at her eyes, dark and wet and beautiful. He kissed her again. "Let's go to my house." His arm went around her shoulders to draw her close to his side.

Driving by, Lindsay passed Andy and Monica and absently lifted her hand in a wave. Neither of them saw her. Her mind crowded with thoughts, she drove on toward the Cliff House. She had to speak with Seth. Time, she felt, was running out for her, for them, for Ruth. Nothing seemed to be going the way it should...not since the afternoon the first snow had stopped.

Seth had gone away almost immediately to his New Zealand site and hadn't returned until a few days before Christmas. He hadn't written or called, and while Lindsay hadn't expected him to, she had hoped for it nonetheless. Missing him was painful. She wanted to be with him again, to recapture some of the happiness, some of the closeness they had shared. Yet she knew that once they had spoken, they could be farther apart than ever. She had to convince him, by whatever means possible, to let Ruth go. Her last conversation with Nick had persuaded her that it was time to press for what was needed, just as it had convinced her it was time to make a final decision about her own life. She wanted Ruth in New York with her.

She took the long curve of Seth's driveway slowly, watching the house as the road rose. Because her heart was thumping inside her chest, she took an extra moment to breathe after she stopped the car. She didn't want to make a fool of herself when she saw Seth again. Ruth's chances depended on her being strong enough to convince him that she knew what the girl needed.

Lindsay got out of the car, nervously clutching her purse in both hands as she walked to the front door. Relax, she told herself. She couldn't allow her feelings for him to ruin what she had come to do.

The wind pinched color into her face, and she was grateful. She had braided her hair and coiled it neatly at her neck so the wind wouldn't disturb it. Composure, at the moment, was vital to her. She knew that the memories of what she had shared with Seth were dormant and would overwhelm her the moment she stepped into the house. She lifted a gloved finger and pushed the doorbell. The wait was mercifully short before Worth answered.

He was dressed much as before. The dark suit and tie were impeccable. The white shirt crisp. The beard was neatly trimmed, his expression inscrutable.

"Good morning, Miss Dunne." There was nothing in his voice to indicate his curiosity at her early call.

"Good morning, Mr. Worth." Lindsay could prevent her hands from nervously twisting her bag, but some of her anxiety escaped into her eyes. "Is Seth in?"

"He's working, I believe, miss." Politely he moved back to allow her entrance into the warmth of the house. "If you'd care to wait in the parlor, I'll see if he can be disturbed."

"Yes, I...please." She bit her lip as she followed his straight back. Don't start babbling, she admonished herself.

"I'll take your coat, miss," he offered as she stepped over the parlor threshold. Wordlessly, Lindsay slipped out of it. The fire was crackling. She could remember making love with Seth here for the first time while the fire hissed and the mantel clock ticked away the time they had together.

"Miss?"

"Yes? Yes, I'm sorry." She turned back to Worth, suddenly aware that he had been speaking to her.

"Would you care for some coffee while you wait?"

"No, nothing. Thank you." She pulled off her gloves and walked to the window. She wanted to regain her composure before Seth joined her. Setting the purse and gloves on a table, she laced her fingers.

It was difficult waiting there, she discovered, in the room where she had first given her love to him. The memories were painfully intimate. Priorities, she reminded herself. I have to remember my priorities. In the window glass she could see just the ghost of her reflection: the trimly cut gray trousers, the burgundy mohair sweater with its full, cuffed sleeves. She looked composed, but the composure, like the woman in the glass, was all illusion.

"Lindsay."

She turned, thinking herself prepared. Seeing him again sent a myriad of feelings washing over her. But the most dominant was an all-encompassing joy. She smiled, filled with it, and crossed the room to him. Her hands sought him without hesitation.

"Seth. It's so good to see you." She felt his hands tighten on hers before he released them to say, "You're looking well," in a casually distant tone that had her battling back the words that trembled on her tongue.

"Thank you." Turning, she walked to the fire, needing to warm herself. "I hope I'm not disturbing you."

"No." Seth stayed where he was. "You're not disturbing me, Lindsay."

"Did things go well in New Zealand?" she asked, facing him again with a more reserved smile. "I imagine the weather was different there."

"A bit," he acknowledged. He moved closer then but kept a safe distance between them. "I have to go back after the first of the year for a few weeks. Things should settle down when that's over. Ruth tells me your house is sold."

"Yes." Lindsay tugged at the collar of her sweater, wishing she had something to fill her hands. "I've moved into the school. Everything changes, doesn't it?" He inclined his head in agreement. "There's plenty of room there, of course, and the house seemed terribly empty when I was alone. It'll be simpler to organize things when I go to New York...."

"You're going to New York?" he interrupted her sharply. Lindsay saw his brows draw together. "When?"

"Next month." She roamed to the window, unable to keep still any longer. "Nick starts staging his ballet then. We reached an agreement on it, finally."

"I see." Seth's words came slowly. He studied the long slope of her neck until she turned back to him. "Then you've decided to go back."

"For one performance." She smiled, trying to pretend it was a casual conversation. Her heart was knocking at her ribs. "The premiere performance is going to be televised. I've agreed, since I was Nick's most publicized partner, to dance the lead for it. The reunion aspect will bring it more attention."

"One performance," Seth mused. He slipped his hands into his pockets as he watched her. "Do you really believe you'll be able to stop at that?"

"Of course," Lindsay tried to say evenly. "I've a number of reasons for doing it. It's important to Nick." She sighed. Thin rays of sunlight passed through the window and fell on her hair. "And it's important to me."

"To see if you can still be a star?"

She lifted her brow with a half-laugh. "No. If I'd had that sort of ego, things would've been different all along. That part of it wasn't ever important enough to me. I suppose that's why my mother and I couldn't agree."

"Don't you think that'll change once you're back living in that kind of world again?" There was an edge to his voice which brought a frown to Lindsay. "When you danced with Davidov in the studio, everything you were was bound up in it."

"Yes, that's as it should be." She closed some of the distance between them, wanting him to understand. "But dancing and performing aren't the same thing always. I've had the performing," she reminded him. "I've had the spotlight. I don't need it anymore."

"Simple enough to say here now. More difficult after you've stood in the spotlight again."

"No." Lindsay shook her head. "It depends on the reasons for going back." She stepped to him, touching the back of his hand with her fingers. "Do you want to know mine?"

He studied her for a long, silent moment, then turned away. "No. No, I don't believe I do." He stood facing the fire. "What if I asked you not to go?"

"Not to go?" Her voice reflected her confusion. She walked to him, laying her hand on his arm. "Why would you?"

Seth turned, and their eyes met. He didn't touch her. "Because I'm in love with you, and I don't want to lose you."

Lindsay's eyes widened. Then she was in his arms, clinging with all her strength. "Kiss me," she demanded. "Before I wake up."

Their lips met with mutual need, tasting and parting to taste again until the sharp edge of hunger had subsided. She pressed her face into his shoulder a moment, hardly daring to believe what she had heard. She felt his hands roam down the softness of her sweater, then under it and upon the softness of her skin.

"I've missed touching you," he murmured. "There were nights I could think of nothing else but your skin."

"Oh, Seth, I can't believe it." She tangled both hands in his hair as she drew her face away from his shoulder. "Tell me again."

He kissed her temple before he drew her close again. "I love you." She felt his body relax as she heard his sigh. "I've never said that to a woman before."

"Not even an Italian countess or a French movie star?" Lindsay's voice was muffled against his throat.

He pulled her away far enough so that their eyes could meet, then he held her there with a look deep and intent. "No one's ever touched me the way you have. I could say I've spent my life looking for someone like you, but I haven't." He smiled, running his hands up her arms until they framed her face. "I didn't know there was anyone like you. You were a surprise."

"That's the nicest thing anyone's ever said to me." She turned her face and kissed the palm of his hand. "When I knew I loved you, I was afraid because it meant needing you so much." She looked at him, and everything in his face pulled at her. He had laid claim not only to her heart and body, but to her mind as well. The depth of it seemed awesome. Suddenly she pressed against him, her pulse speeding wildly. "Hold me," she whispered, shutting her eyes. "I'm still afraid."

Her mouth sought his, and the kiss that ensued was electric. They took each other deep until neither could rise to the surface alone. It was a kiss of total dependence. They held each other and gave.

"I've been half-alive since you walked out of the studio that day," she confessed. The planes of his face demanded the exploration of her fingertips. "Everything's been flat, like the photograph of the snow would have been."

"I couldn't stay. You had told me that what had happened between us had been nice. Two adults, alone, attracted to each other. Very simple." He shook his head, pulling her closer possessively. "That caught me by the throat. I loved you, I needed you. For the first time in my life, it wasn't simple."

"Can't you tell when someone's lying?" she asked softly.

"Not when I'm trying to deal with being in love."

"If I had known..." Her voice trailed as she nestled, listening to the sound of his heartbeat.

"I wanted to tell you, but then I watched you dance. You were so exquisite, so perfect." He breathed in her scent again, holding her close. "I hated it. Every second I watched you go further away."

"No, Seth." She silenced him with her fingertips on his lips. "It's not like that. It's not like that at all."

"Isn't it?" He took her by the shoulders, holding her away. "He was offering you a life you could never share with me. He was offering you your place in the lights again. I told myself I had to do the right thing and let you walk away. I've stayed away from you all these weeks. But I knew the moment I saw you standing here today that I couldn't let you go."

"You don't understand." Her eyes were sad and pleading. "I don't want that life again, or the place in the lights, even if I could have it. That's not why I'm going back to do this ballet."

"I don't want you to go." His fingers tightened on her shoulders. "I'm asking you not to go."

She studied him for a moment with all the emotion still brimming in her eyes. "What if I asked you not to go to New Zealand?"

Abruptly he released her and turned away. "That's not the same thing. It's my job. In a few weeks it would be over and I'd be back. It's not a life-ruling force." When he turned back to her, his hands were balled in his pockets. "Would there be room for me and for children in your life if you were prima ballerina with the company?"

"Perhaps not." She came closer but knew from the look in his eyes that she dared not touch him. "But I'll never be prima ballerina with the company. If I wanted it with all my heart, it still couldn't be. And I don't want it. Why can't you understand? I simply haven't the need for it. I won't even officially be with the company for this performance. I'll have guest status."

This time it was she who turned away, too filled with emotions to be still. "I want to do it, for Nick, because he's my friend. Our bond is very special. And for myself. I'll be able to close out this chapter of my life with something beautiful instead of my father's death. That's important to me; I didn't know myself how important until recently. I have to do it, or else I'd live forever with regrets."

In the silence a log shifted and spewed sparks against the screen.

"So you'll go, no matter how I feel."

Lindsay turned slowly. Her eyes were dry and direct. "I'll go, and I'll ask you to trust me. And I want to take Ruth."

"No." His answer came immediately and with an edge. "You ask for too much. You ask for too damn much."

"It isn't too much," she countered. "Listen to me. Nick asked for her. He watched her dance; he tested her here, and he wants her. She could have a place in the *corps* by summer, Seth, she's that good. Don't hold her back."

"Don't talk to me about holding her back." Fury licked at the words. "You've described to me the life she'd lead, the physical pain and emotional anguish, the pressures, the demands. She's a child. She doesn't need that."

"Yes, she does." Lindsay paced back to him. "She's not a child; she's a young woman, and she needs it all if she's going to be a dancer. You haven't the right to deny her this."

"I have every right."

Lindsay breathed deeply, trying to keep control. "Legally, your right will run out in a few months. Then you'll put her into a position of having to go against your wishes. She'll be miserably unhappy about that, and it could be too late for her. Nikolai Davidov doesn't volunteer to train every young dancer he runs across. Ruth is special."

"Don't tell me about Ruth!" His voice rose, surprising her. "It's

181

taken nearly a year for her to begin to be happy again. I won't push her into the kind of world where she has to punish herself every day just to keep up. If it's what you want, then take it. I can't stop you." He took her by the arm and pulled her to him. "But you won't live out your career vicariously through Ruth."

Color fled from Lindsay's face. Her eyes were huge and blue and incredulous. "Is that what you think of me?" she whispered.

"I don't know what I think of you." His face was as alive with fury as hers was cold with shock. "I don't understand you. I can't keep you here; loving you isn't enough. But Ruth's another matter. You won't keep your spotlight through her, Lindsay. You'll have to fight for that yourself."

"Let me go, please." This time it was she who possessed the restraint and control. Though she trembled, her voice was utterly calm. When Seth had released her, she stood for a moment, studying him. "Everything I've told you today is the truth. Everything. Would you please have Worth bring my coat now? I have classes very soon." She turned to the fire; her back was very straight. "I don't think we have anything more to say to each other."

Chapter 14

It was very different being the student rather than the teacher. Most of the women in Lindsay's classes were years younger than her; girls, really. Those who had reached their mid- and late twenties had been on the professional circuit all along. She worked hard. The days were very long and made the nights easier to bear.

The hours were filled with classes, then rehearsals and yet more classes. She roomed with two members of the company who had been friends during her professional days. At night she slept deeply, her mind dazed with fatigue. In the morning her classes took over her body. Her muscles grew familiar with aches and cramps again as January became February. The routine was the same as it had always been: impossible.

The studio window was darkened by an ice storm, but no one seemed to notice as they rehearsed a dance from the first act of Davidov's *Ariel*. The music was fairylike, conjuring up scenes of dusky forests and wild flowers. It was here that the young prince would meet Ariel. Mortal and Sprite would fall in love. The *pas de deux* was difficult, demanding on the female lead because of its combinations of *soubresauts* and *jetés*. High-level energy was required while keeping the moves light and ethereal. Near the end of the scene, Lindsay was to leap away from Nikolai, turning in the air as she did so in order to be facing him, teasingly, when she touched ground again. Her landing was shaky, and she was forced to plant both feet to prevent a spill. Nick cursed vividly.

"I'm sorry." Her breath came quickly after the exertion of the dance.

"Apologies!" He emphasized his anger with a furious flick of his hand. "I can't dance with an apology."

Other dancers in the room glared at Lindsay with varying degrees of sympathy. All of them had felt the rough edge of Davidov's tongue. The pianist automatically flipped back to the beginning of the suite.

Lindsay's body ached from a twelve-hour, punishing day. "My feet hardly touch the ground in the whole third scene," she tossed back at him. Someone handed her a towel, and gratefully she wiped sweat from her neck and brow. "I haven't got wings, Nick."

"Obviously."

It amazed her that his sarcasm wounded. Usually it touched off anger, and the row that would ensue would clear the air. Now she felt it necessary to defend herself. "It's difficult," she murmured, pushing loosened wisps of hair behind her ear.

"Difficult!" He roared at her, crossing the room to stand in front of her. "So it is difficult. Did I bring you here to watch you do a simple pirouette across the stage?" His hair curled damply around his face as his eyes blazed at her.

"You didn't bring me," she corrected, but her voice was shaky, without its usual strength. "I came."

"You came." He turned away with a wide gesture. "To dance like a truck driver."

The sob came too quickly for her to prevent it. Appalled, she pressed her hands to her face. She had just enough time to see the stunned look on Nikolai's face before she fled the room.

Lindsay let the door to the rest room slam behind her. In the far corner was a low bench. Lindsay curled up on it and wept as if her heart would break. Unable to cope any longer, she let the hurt pour out. Her sobs bounced off the walls and came back to her. When an arm slipped around her, Lindsay turned into it, accepting the offered comfort blindly. She needed someone.

Nikolai rocked and stroked her until the passion of her tears lessened. She had curled into him like a child, and he held her close, murmuring in Russian.

"My little dove." Gently he kissed her temple. "I've been cruel."

"Yes." She used the towel she had draped over her shoulders to dry her eyes. She was drained, empty, and if the pain was still there, she was too numb to feel it.

"But always before, you fight back." He tilted her chin. Her eyes were brilliant and wet. "We are very volatile, yes?" Nikolai smiled, kissing the corners of her mouth. "I yell at you, you yell at me, then we dance."

To their mutual distress, Lindsay buried her face in his shoulder and began to cry again. "I don't know why I'm acting this way." She took deep breaths to stop herself. "I hate people who act this way. It just all seems so crazy. Sometimes it feels like it's three years ago and nothing's changed. Then I see girls like Allyson Gray." Lindsay sniffed, thinking of the dancer who would take over the part of Ariel. "She's twelve years old."

"Twenty," Nikolai corrected, patting her hair.

"She makes me feel forty. And the classes seem hours longer than they ever did before."

"You're doing beautifully; you know that." He hugged her and kissed the top of her head.

"I feel like a clod," she said miserably. "An uncoordinated clod."

Nikolai smiled into her hair but kept his voice sympathetic. "You've lost the five pounds."

"Six," she corrected, and sighing, wiped her eyes again. "Who has time to eat? I'll probably keep on shrinking until I disappear." She glanced around, then her eyes widened. "Nick, you can't be in here, this is the ladies' room."

"I'm Davidov," he said imperially. "I go anywhere."

That made her laugh, and she kissed him. "I feel like a total fool. I've never fallen apart at a rehearsal like that before."

"It's not any of the things we talked about." He took her shoulders, and now his look was solemn. "It's the architect."

"No," she said too quickly. Only his left brow moved. "Yes." She let out a long breath and closed her eyes. "Yes."

"Will you talk about it now?"

Opening her eyes, Lindsay nodded. She settled back in the curve of his shoulder and let the silence hang for a moment. "He told me he loved me," she began. "I thought, this is what I've waited for all my life. He loves me, and life's going to be perfect. But love isn't enough. I didn't know that, but it's not. Understanding, trust...love is a closed hand without those."

She paused in silence, remembering clearly every moment of her last meeting with Seth. Nikolai waited for her to continue. "He couldn't deal with my coming back for this ballet. He couldn't—or wouldn't—understand that I had to do it. He wouldn't trust me when I told him it was only for this one time. He wouldn't believe that I didn't want this life again, that I wanted to build one with him. He asked me not to go."

186

"That was selfish," Nikolai stated. He frowned at the wall and moved Lindsay closer to him. "He's a selfish man."

She smiled, thinking how simple it had been for Nick to demand that she come. It seemed she was caught between two selfish men. "Yes. But perhaps there should be some selfishness in love. I don't know." She was calm now, her breathing steady. "If he had believed me, believed that I wasn't going back to a life that would exclude him, we might have come to an understanding."

"Might?"

"There's Ruth." A new weight seemed to drag on her heart. "There was nothing I could say that would convince him to send her here. Nothing that could make him see that he was depriving her of everything she was, everything she could be. We argued about her often, most violently the last time I saw him."

Lindsay swallowed, feeling some of the pain return. "He loves her very much and takes his responsibility for her very seriously. He didn't want her to deal with the hardships of the life we lead here. He thinks she's too young, and..." Lindsay was interrupted by a Russian curse she recognized. It lightened her mood a little, and she relaxed against him again. "You'd see it that way, of course, but for an outsider, things look differently."

"There is only one way," he began.

"Davidov's," Lindsay supplied, adoring him for his perfect confidence.

"Naturally," he agreed, but she heard the humor in his voice.

"A non-dancer might disagree," she murmured. "I understand how he feels, and that makes it harder, I suppose, because I know, regardless of that, that Ruth belongs here. He feels..." She bit her lip, remembering. "He thinks I want to use her, to continue my career through her. That was the worst of it."

187

Davidov remained silent for several moments, digesting all Lindsay had told him, then adding it to his own impressions of Seth Bannion. "I think it was a man very hurt who would say that to you."

"I never saw him again after that. We left each other hurting."

"You'll go back in the spring, when your dance is over." He tilted her face. "You'll see him then."

"I don't know. I don't know if I can." Her eyes were tragic. "Perhaps it's best to leave things as they are, so we don't hurt each other again."

"Love hurts, *ptichka*," he said with a broad shrug. "The ballet hurts you, your lover hurts you. Life. Now, wash your face," he told her briskly. "It's time to dance again."

Lindsay faced herself at the barre. She was alone now in a practice room five stories above Manhattan. It was night, and the windows were black. On the CD player, the music came slowly, a piano only. Turning out, she began to lift her right leg. It seemed straight from the hip to the toe, one long line. Keeping her eyes locked on her eyes in the mirror, she took the leg behind her into an *attitude* position, then rose slowly onto her toe. She held it firm, refusing to let her muscles quiver, then brought her leg back painstakingly on the return journey. She repeated the exercise with her left leg.

It had been nearly a week since her outburst at rehearsal. Every night since then she had used the practice room when everyone had gone. An extra hour of reminding her body what was expected of it, an extra hour of keeping her mind from drifting back to Seth. *Glissade, assemblé, changement, changement.* Her mind ordered, and her body obeyed. In six weeks she would be performing for the first time in more than three years. For the last time in her life. She would be ready.

She took herself into an achingly slow *grand plié,* aware of each tendon. Her leotard was damp from her efforts. As she rose again, a movement in the mirror broke her concentration. She would have sworn at the interruption, but then her vision focused.

"Ruth?" She turned just as the girl rushed toward her. Enveloped in a tight hug, Lindsay was thrown back to the first time they had met. She had touched Ruth's shoulder and had been rejected. How far she's come, Lindsay thought, returning the hug with all her strength. "Let me look at you." Drawing away, Lindsay framed her face. It was animated, laughing, the eyes dark and bright. "You look wonderful. Wonderful."

"I missed you. I missed you so much!"

"What are you doing here?" Lindsay took her hands, automatically chafing the cold from them. "Seth. Is Seth with you?" Hoping, fearing, she looked to the doorway.

"No, he's at home." Ruth saw the answer to the question she harbored. She was still in love with him. "He couldn't get away right now."

"I see." Lindsay brought her attention back to Ruth and managed a smile. "But how did you get here? And why?"

"I came by train," Ruth answered. "To study ballet."

"To study?" Lindsay became very still. "I don't understand."

"Uncle Seth and I had a long talk a few weeks ago before he went back to New Zealand." She unzipped her corduroy jacket and slipped out of it. "Right after you'd left for New York, actually."

"A talk?" Lindsay moved to the CD player to switch off the music. She used a towel to dry her neck, then left it draped over her shoulders. "What about?"

"About what I wanted in my life, what was important to me and why." She watched Lindsay carefully remove the CD from the player.

189

She could see the nerves in the movements. "He had a lot of reservations about letting me come here. I guess you know that."

"Yes, I know." Lindsay slipped the disc back into its case.

"He wanted what was best for me. After my parents were killed, I had a hard time adjusting to things. The first couple of months, he dropped everything just to be with me when I needed him. And even after, I know he rearranged his life, his work, for me." Ruth laid her coat over the back of a wooden chair. "He's been so good to me."

Lindsay nodded, unable to speak. The wound was opening again.

"I know it was hard for him to let me come, to let me make the choice. He's been wonderful about it, taking care of all the paperwork with school, and he arranged for me to stay with a family he knows. They have a really great duplex on the East Side. They let me bring Nijinsky." She walked to the barre, and in jeans and sneakers, began to exercise.

"It's so wonderful here." Her expression shone radiant as Lindsay watched it in the glass. "And Mr. Davidov said he'd work with me in the evenings when he has time."

"You've seen Nick?" Lindsay crossed over so that they both stood at the barre.

"About an hour ago. I was trying to find you." She smiled, her head dipping below Lindsay's as she bent her knees. "He said I'd find you here, that you come every evening to practice. I can hardly wait until the ballet. He said I could watch it from backstage if I wanted."

"And, of course, you do." Lindsay touched her hair, then walked to the bench to change her shoes.

"Aren't you terribly excited?" Ruth did three *pirouettes* to join her. "Dancing the lead in Davidov's first ballet."

"Once," Lindsay reminded her, undoing the satin ribbons on her shoes.

"Opening night," Ruth countered. Clasping her hands together, Ruth looked down at Lindsay. "How will you be able to give it up again?"

"It's not again," she corrected. "It's *still*. This is a favor for a friend, and for myself." She winced, slipping the shoe from her foot.

"Hurt?"

"Oh, God, yes."

Ruth dropped to her knees and began to work Lindsay's toes. She could feel the tension in them. With a sigh Lindsay laid her head against the wall and closed her eyes.

"Uncle Seth's going to try to come spend a few days with me in the spring. He isn't happy."

"He'll miss you." The cramps in Lindsay's feet were subsiding slowly.

"I don't mean about that."

The words caused Lindsay to open her eyes. Ruth was watching her solemnly, though her fingers still worked at the pain. "Did he say anything? Did he send a message?"

Ruth shook her head. Lindsay shut her eyes again.

Chapter 15

Lindsay found that a three-year absence hadn't made her any less frantic during the hours before a performance. For the past two weeks she had endured hours of interviews and photography sessions, questions and answers and flashing cameras. The reunion of Dunne and Davidov for a one-time performance of a ballet he himself had written and choreographed was news. For Nick and for the company, Lindsay made herself available for any publicity required. Unfortunately, it added to the already impossibly long days.

The performance was a benefit, and the audience would be star-studded. The ballet would be televised, and all proceeds would be donated to a scholarship fund for gifted young dancers. Publicity could encourage yet more donations. For this, Lindsay wanted success.

If the ballet was well-received, it would be incorporated into the program for the season. Nick would broaden himself immeasurably in the world of dance. For him, and for herself, Lindsay wanted success.

There had been a phone call from her mother and a visit from

Ruth in her dressing room. The phone call had had a warm tone, without pressures.

Mae was as pleased about the upcoming performance as she could have been; but to Lindsay's surprise and delight, her own responsibilities and new life demanded that she remain in California. Her heart and thoughts would be there with Lindsay, she promised, and she would view the ballet on television.

The visit from Ruth had been a breath of fresh air. Ruth had become star-struck at the mechanics of backstage life. She was a willing slave for anyone who asked. Next year, Lindsay thought, watching her bustle about carrying costumes and props, she would be fussing over her own costumes.

Taking a hammer, she took a new pair of toe shoes, sat on the floor and began to pound them. She would make them supple before sewing on the ribbons. Her costumes hung in order in the closet. Backstage cacophony accompanied the sound of hammer against wood. There was makeup and hair styling yet to be seen to, and dressing in the white tutu for the first act. Lindsay went through each process, aware of the video cameras that were recording the preperformance stage of the ballet. Only her warmups were done in private, at her insistence. Here, she would begin to focus the concentration she would need to carry her through the following hours.

The pressure in her chest was building as she walked down the corridor toward the wings at stage left. Here, she would make her entrance after the opening dance by the forest ensemble. The music and lights were already on her. She knew Nick would be waiting in the wings at stage right, anticipating his own entrance. Ruth stood beside her, gently touching her wrist as if to wish her luck without speaking the words. Superstitions never die in the theater. Lindsay watched the dancers, the women in their long, bell-like white dresses, the men in their vests and tunics.

Twenty bars, then fifteen, and she began taking long, slow breaths. Ten bars and then five. Her throat went dry. The knot in her stomach threatened to become genuine nausea. The cold film on her skin was terror. She closed her eyes briefly, then ran onto the stage.

At her entrance, the rising applause was a welcome wave. Lindsay never heard it. For her, there was only the music. Her movements flowed with the joy of the first scene. The dance was short but strenuous, and when she ran back into the wings, beads of moisture clung to her brow. She allowed herself to be patted dry and fed a stingy sip of water as she watched Nick take over the second scene. Within seconds, he had the audience in the palm of his hand.

"Oh yes," Lindsay breathed, then turned to smile at Ruth. "It's going to be perfect."

The ballet revolved around its principals, and it was rare for one or both of them not to be onstage. In the final scene the music slowed and the lights became a misty blue. Lindsay wore a floating knee-length gown. It was here that Ariel had to decide whether to give up her immortality for love; to marry the prince, she had to become mortal and renounce all her magic.

Lindsay danced alone in the moonlit forest, recalling the joy and simplicity of her life with the trees and flowers. To have love— mortal love—she had to turn her back on everything she had known. The choice brought great sadness. Even as she despaired, falling on the ground to weep, the prince entered the forest. He knelt beside her, touching her shoulder to bring her face to his.

The *grand pas de deux* expressed his love for her, his need to have her beside him. She was drawn to him, yet afraid of losing the life she had always known, afraid of facing death as a mortal. She soared with freedom, through the trees and the moonlight that had always been hers, but again and again, she was pulled back to him by her own heart. She stopped, for dawn was breaking, and the time for decision had come.

He reached out to her, but she turned away, uncertain, frightened. In despair, he started to leave her. At the last moment, she called him back. The first rays of sunlight seeped through the trees as she ran to him. He lifted her into his arms as she gave him her heart and her life.

The curtain had closed, but still Nick held her. Their pulses were soaring, and for the moment, they had eyes only for each other.

"Thank you." And he kissed her softly, as a friend saying goodbye.

"Nick." Her eyes filled with emotion after emotion, but he set her down before she could speak.

"Listen," he ordered, gesturing to the closed curtain. The sound of applause battered against it. "We can't keep them waiting forever."

Flowers and people. It seemed that no more of either could be crammed into Lindsay's dressing room. There was laughter, and someone poured her a glass of champagne. She set it down untasted. Her mind was already drunk with the moment. She answered questions and smiled, but nothing seemed completely in focus. She was still in costume and makeup, still part Ariel.

There were men in tuxedos and women in sparkling evening dress mingling with elves and wood sprites. She had spoken to an actor of star magnitude and a visiting French dignitary. All she could do was hope her responses had been coherent. When she spotted Ruth, Lindsay hailed her, the look in her eyes entreating.

"Stay with me, will you?" she asked when the girl managed to plow her way through the crowd. "I'm not normal yet; I need someone."

"Oh, Lindsay." Ruth threw her arms around her neck. "You were so wonderful! I've never seen anything more wonderful."

Lindsay laughed and returned the hug. "Just bring me down. I'm still in the air." She was interrupted by the assistant director, who brought more flowers and champagne.

It was more than an hour before the crowd thinned. By then, Lindsay was feeling the weariness that follows an emotional high. It was Nick, who had managed to work his way out of his own dressing room to find her, who cleared the room. Seeing the telltale signs of fatigue on her face, he reminded those remaining of a reception being held at a nearby restaurant.

"You must go so *ptichka* can change," he said jovially, patting a back and nudging it out the door. "Save us some champagne. And caviar," he added, "if it's Russian."

Within five minutes, only he and Ruth joined Lindsay in the flower-filled room.

"So," he addressed Ruth, coming over to pinch her chin. "You think your teacher did well tonight?"

"Oh, yes." Ruth smiled at Lindsay. "She did beautifully."

"I mean me." He tossed back his hair and looked insulted.

"You weren't too bad," Lindsay informed him.

"Not too bad?" He sniffed, rising to his full height. "Ruth, I would ask you to leave us a moment. This lady and I have something to discuss."

"Of course."

Before Ruth could step away, Lindsay took her hand. "Wait." From her dressing table she took a rose, one that had been thrown at her feet after the performance. She handed it to Ruth. "To a new Ariel, another day."

Wordlessly, Ruth looked down at the rose, then at Lindsay. Her eyes were eloquent, though she could only nod her thanks before she left the room.

"Ah, my little bird," Nick took her hand and kissed it. "Such a good heart."

She squeezed his fingers in return. "But you will cast her in it. Three years, perhaps two."

He nodded. "There are some who are made for such things." His eyes met hers. "I will never dance with a more perfect Ariel than I have tonight."

Lindsay leaned forward so that their faces were close. "Charm, Nick, for me? I had thought I was through with bouquets tonight."

"I love you, *ptichka*."

"I love you, Nicky."

"Will you do me one last favor?"

She smiled, leaning back in her chair again. "How could I refuse?"

"There is someone else I would like you to see tonight."

She gave him a look of good-humored weariness. "I can only pray it's not another reporter. I'll see whomever you like," she agreed recklessly. "As long as you don't expect me to go to that reception."

"You are excused," he said with a regal inclination of his head. He went to the door, and opening it, turned briefly to look at her.

She sat, obviously exhausted in the chair. Her hair flowed freely over the shoulders of the thin white gown, her eyes exotic with their exaggerated lines and coloring. She smiled at him, but he left without speaking again.

Briefly, Lindsay closed her eyes, but almost instantly a tingle ran up her spine. Her throat went dry as it had before her first dance of the ballet. She knew who would be there when she opened her eyes.

She rose when Seth closed the door behind him, but slowly, as if measuring the distance between them. She was alert again, sharply, completely, as if she had awakened from a long, restful sleep. She was suddenly aware of the powerful scent of flowers and the masses of color they brought to the room. She was aware that his face was thinner but that he stood straight and his eyes were still direct and serious. She was aware that her love for him hadn't lessened by a single degree.

"Hello." She tried to smile. Formal clothing suited him, she decided as she laced her fingers together. She remembered, too, how right he had looked in jeans and a flannel shirt. There are so many Seth Bannions, she mused. And I love them all.

"You were magnificent," he said. He came no closer to her but stood, seeming to draw every inch of her through his eyes. "But I suppose you've heard that too often tonight."

"Never too often," she returned. "And not from you." She wanted to cross the room to him, but the hurt was still there, and the distance was so far. "I didn't know you were coming."

"I asked Ruth not to say anything." He came farther into the room, but the gap still seemed immense. "I didn't come to see you before the performance because I thought it might upset you. It didn't seem fair."

"You sent her…I'm glad."

"I was wrong about that." He lifted a single rose from a table and studied it a moment. "You were right, she belongs here. I was wrong about a great many things."

"I was wrong, too, to try to push you too soon." Lindsay unlaced her fingers, then helplessly, she laced them again. "Ruth needed what you were giving her. I don't think she'd be the person she is right now if you hadn't had those months with her. She's happy now."

"And you?" He looked up again and pinned her with his gaze. "Are you?"

She opened her mouth to speak, and finding no words, turned away. There on the dressing table was a half-filled bottle of champagne and her untouched glass. Lindsay lifted the glass and drank. The bubbles soothed the tightness in her throat. "Would you like some champagne? I seem to have plenty."

"Yes." He took the last steps toward her. "I would."

Nervous now that he stood so close, Lindsay looked around for another glass. "Silly," she said, keeping her back to him. "I don't seem to have a clean glass anywhere."

"I'll share yours." He laid a hand on her shoulder, gently turning her to face him. He placed his fingers over hers on the stem. He drank, keeping his eyes on hers.

"Nothing's any good without you." Her voice broke as he lowered the glass. "Nothing."

His fingers tightened on hers, and she saw something flash in his eyes. "Don't forgive me too quickly, Lindsay," he advised. The contact was broken when he placed the glass back on the table. "The things I said…"

"No. No, they don't matter now." Her eyes filled and brimmed over.

"They do," he corrected quietly. "To me. I was afraid of losing you and pushed you right out of my life."

"I've never been out of your life."

She would have gone to him then, but he turned away. "You're a terrifying person to be in love with, Lindsay, so warm, so giving. I've never known anyone like you." When he turned back, she could see the emotions in his eyes, not so controlled now, not so contained. "I've never needed anyone before, and then I needed you and felt you slipping away."

"But I wasn't." She was in his arms before he could say another word. When he stiffened, she lifted her face and found his mouth. Instantly, the kiss became avid and deep. The low sound of his breath sent pleasure through her. "Seth. Oh, Seth, I've been half-alive for three months. Don't leave me again."

Holding her close, he breathed in the scent of her hair. "You left me," he murmured.

"I won't again." She lifted her face so that her eyes, huge and brilliant, promised him. "Not ever again."

"Lindsay." He reached up to frame her face. "I can't...I won't ask you to give up what you have here. Watching you tonight..."

"You don't have to ask me anything." She placed her hands on his wrists, willing him to believe her. "Why can't you understand? This isn't what I want. Not now, not anymore. I want you. I want a home and a family."

He looked at her deeply, then shook his head. "It's difficult to believe you can walk away from this. You must have heard that applause."

She smiled. It should be so simple, she thought. "Seth, I pushed myself for three months. I worked harder than I've ever worked in my life to give one performance. I'm tired; I want to go home. Marry me. Share my life."

With a sigh, he rested his forehead on hers. "No one's ever proposed to me before."

"Good, then I'm the first." It was so easy to melt in his arms.

"And the last," he murmured between kisses.

* * * * *

Keep reading for a sneak peek
at Nora Roberts' latest story,
Legacy . . .

CHAPTER ONE

GEORGETOWN

The first time Adrian Rizzo met her father, he tried to kill her.

At seven, her world consisted primarily of movement. Most of the time she lived with her mother—and Mimi, who looked after them both—in New York. But sometimes they stayed in L.A. for a few weeks, or in Chicago or Miami.

In the summer, she got to visit with her grandparents in Maryland for at least two weeks. That, in her opinion, was the most fun because they had dogs and a big yard to play in, and a tire for a swing.

When they lived in Manhattan, she went to school, and that was fine. She got to take dance lessons, and do gymnastics, and that was way better than school.

When they traveled for her mother's work, Mimi homeschooled her because she had to be educated. Mimi made learning about the place they stayed part of being educated. Since they were in DC for a whole month, part of school meant visiting the monuments, taking a White House tour, and going to the Smithsonian.

Sometimes she got to work with her mom, and she liked that a lot. Whenever she got to work in one of her mom's fitness videos, she had to learn a routine, like a cardio dance or yoga poses.

She liked learning; she liked dancing.

At five, she did a whole video with her mom geared toward kids and families. A yoga one because, after all, she *was* the baby in Yoga Baby, her mother's company.

It made her proud, and excited that her mother said they'd do another. Maybe when she was ten to target that age group.

Her mom knew all about age groups and demographics and things like that. Adrian heard her talking about them with her manager and her producers.

Her mom knew plenty about fitness, too, and the mind-body connection, and nutrition, and meditation, and all sorts of things like that.

She didn't know how to cook—not like Popi and Nonna, who owned a restaurant. She didn't like to play games like Mimi—because she stayed really busy building her career.

She had a lot of meetings, and rehearsals, and planning sessions, and public appearances, and interviews.

Even at seven, Adrian understood Lina Rizzo didn't know a whole lot about being a mom.

Still, she didn't mind if Adrian played with her makeup—as long as she put everything back where it belonged. And she never got mad if they worked on a routine and Adrian made mistakes.

Best of all on this trip, instead of flying back to New York when her mom finished this video and all the interviews and meetings, they got to drive to visit her grandparents for a long weekend.

She had plans to try to negotiate that into a week, but for now she sat on the floor in the doorway and watched her mother work out another routine.

Lina had chosen this house for the month because it had a home gym with mirrored walls, something as essential to her as the number of bedrooms.

She did squats and lunges, knee lifts, burpees—Adrian knew all the names. And Lina talked to the mirror—her viewers—giving instructions, encouragement.

Now and then she said a bad word and started something over again.

Adrian thought her beautiful, like a sweaty princess, even though she didn't have her makeup on because there weren't any people or cameras. She had green eyes like Nonna and skin that looked like she bathed in the sun—even though she didn't. Her hair—pulled back in a scrunchie now—was like the chestnuts you could buy all warm and smelling good in a bag at Christmastime.

She was tall—not as tall as Popi—and Adrian hoped she would be, too, when she grew up.

She wore tight, tiny shorts and a sports bra—but she wouldn't wear anything that showed so much for videos or appearances because Lina said it wasn't classy.

Since she'd been raised to be mind-body-health conscious, Adrian knew her mom was fit, firm, and fabulous.

Muttering to herself, Lina walked over to make some notes on what Adrian knew was the outline for the video. This one would include three segments—cardio, strength training, and yoga—each thirty minutes, with a bonus fifteen-minute express section on total body.

Lina grabbed a towel to mop off her face and spotted her daughter.

"Crap, Adrian! You gave me a jolt. I didn't know you were there. Where's Mimi?"

"She's in the kitchen. We're going to have chicken and rice and asparagus for dinner."

"Great. Why don't you go give her a hand with that? I need a shower."

"How come you're mad?"

"I'm not mad."

"You were mad when you were talking on the phone with Harry. You yelled how you didn't tell anybody, especially some bad-word tabloid reporter."

Lina yanked the scrunchie out of her hair the way she did when she had a headache. "You shouldn't listen to private conversations."

"I didn't listen, I *heard*. Are you mad at Harry?"

Adrian really liked her mother's publicist. He snuck her little bags of M&M's or Skittles and told funny jokes.

"No, I'm not mad at Harry. Go help Mimi. Tell her I'll be down in about a half hour."

She was, too, mad, Adrian thought when her mother walked away. Maybe not at Harry, but at somebody, because she'd made a lot of mistakes when she'd practiced and said a lot of bad words.

Her mother hardly ever made mistakes.

Or maybe she just had a headache. Mimi said people sometimes got headaches if they worried too much.

Adrian got up from the floor. But since helping with dinner was boring, she went into the fitness room. She stood in front of the mirrors, a girl tall for her age with her curly hair—black as her grandfather's had once been—escaping a green scrunchie. Her eyes had too much gold in them to rate a true green like her mother's, but she kept hoping they'd change.

In her pink shorts and flowered T-shirt, she struck a pose. And turning on the music in her head, danced.

She loved her dance classes *and* gymnastics when they were in New York, but now she imagined not taking a class, but leading one.

She twirled, kicked, did a handspring, the splits. Cross-step, salsa, *leap!* Making it up as she went.

She amused herself for twenty minutes. The last innocent twenty minutes of her life.

Then someone pushed the buzzer on the front door. And kept pushing it.

It had an angry sound, and one she'd never forget.

She wasn't supposed to open the door herself, but that didn't mean she couldn't go see. So she wandered out to the living room, then the entranceway as Mimi marched in from the kitchen.

Mimi dried her hands on a bright red dishcloth as she hustled through. "For Pete's sake! Where's the fire?"

She rolled her deep brown eyes at Adrian, tucked the cloth in the waistband of her jeans.

A small woman with a powerful voice, she shouted, "Hold your damn horses!"

She knew Mimi was the same age as her mother because they'd gone to college together.

"What's your problem?" she snapped, then turned the lock and opened the door.

From where she stood, Adrian saw Mimi's expression go from irritated—like it got when Adrian didn't pick up her room—to scared.

And everything happened so fast.

Mimi tried to close the door again, but the man pushed it open, pushed her back. He was big, so much bigger than Mimi. He had a little beard with some gray in it, and more in his hair, like silver wings on the gold, but his face was all red like he'd been running. Adrian's first shock at seeing the big man shove Mimi froze her in place.

"Where the fuck is she?"

"She's not here. You can't barge in here like this. Get out. You get out now, Jon, or I'm calling the police."

"Lying bitch." He grabbed Mimi's arm, shook her. "Where is she? She thinks she can run her mouth, ruin my *life*?"

"Get your hands off me. You're drunk."

When she tried to pull away, he slapped her. The sound reverberated like a gunshot in Adrian's head, and she leapt forward.

"Don't you hit her! You leave her alone!"

"Adrian, you go upstairs. Go upstairs right now."

But temper up, Adrian balled her fists. "He has to go away!"

"For this?" the man snarled at Adrian. "For this she ruins my goddamn life? Doesn't look a thing like me. She must've been whoring around, and she's trying to pin the little bastard on me. Fuck that. Fuck her."

"Adrian, upstairs." Mimi whirled toward her, and Adrian didn't see mad—like what she felt. She saw scared. "*Now!*"

"The bitch is up there, isn't she? Liar. Here's what I do to liars." He didn't slap this time, but used his fist, once, twice, on Mimi's face.

When she crumpled, that fear dove into Adrian. Help. She had to get help.

But he caught her on the stairs, snapped her head back as he grabbed the tail of curly hair and yanked.

She screamed, screamed for her mother.

"Yeah, you call Mommy." He slapped her so the sting burned like fire in her face. "We want to talk to Mommy."

As he dragged her up the stairs, Lina ran out of the bedroom in a robe, her hair still wet from the shower.

"Adrian Rizzo, what the—"

She stopped, stood very still as she locked eyes with the man. "Let her go, Jon. Let her go so you and I can talk."

"You've done enough talking. You ruined my life, you stupid hick."

"I didn't talk to that reporter—or to anyone about you. That story didn't come from me."

"Liar!" He yanked Adrian's hair again, so hard it felt like her head was on fire.

Lina took two careful steps forward. "Let her go, and we'll work it out. I can fix this."

"Too fucking late. The university suspended me this morning. My wife is mortified. My children—and I don't believe for one fucking minute this little bitch is mine—are crying. You came back here, back to *my* city, to do this."

"No, Jon. I came for work. I didn't talk to the reporter. It's been over seven years, Jon, why would I do this now? At all? You're hurting my daughter. Stop hurting my daughter."

"He hit Mimi." Adrian could smell her mother's shower and shampoo—the subtle sweetness of orange blossoms. And the stink from the man she didn't know was sweat and bourbon. "He hit her in the face, and she fell down."

"What have you . . ." Lina took her eyes off him to look over the railing that ran across the second floor. She saw Mimi, face bloody, crawling behind a sofa.

She tracked her gaze back to Jon. "You have to stop this, Jon, before someone gets hurt. Let me—"

"I'm hurt, you fucking whore!"

His voice sounded hot and red, like his face, like the fire burning in Adrian's scalp.

"I'm sorry this happened, but—"

"My family's hurt! Want to see some hurt? Let's start with your bastard."

He threw her. Adrian had the sensation of flying, brief and terrifying, before she hit the edge of the top step. The fire that had been in her head now burst in her wrist, her hand, flared up her arm. Then her head banged against the wood, and all she could see was her mother as the man lurched toward her.

He hit her, he hit her, but her mother hit back, and kicked. And there were terrible sounds, so terrible she wanted to cover her ears, but she couldn't move, could only sprawl on the steps and shake.

Even when her mother shouted at her to run, she couldn't.

He had his hands around her mother's throat, shaking her, and her mom hit him in the face, like he had Mimi.

There was blood, there was blood, on her mom, on the man.

They were holding each other, almost like a hug, but hard and mean. Then her mother stomped down on his foot, jerked her knee up. And when the man stumbled back, she shoved.

He hit the railing. Then he was flying.

Adrian saw him fall, arms waving. She saw him crash into the table where her mother put flowers and candles. She heard those terrible sounds. She saw the blood run out from his head, his ears, his nose.

She saw . . .

Then her mother lifted her, turned her, pressed her face to her breast.

"Don't look, Adrian. It's all right now."

"It hurts."

"I know." Lina cradled Adrian's wrist. "I'm going to fix it. Mimi. Oh, Mimi."

"The police are coming." Her eye swollen, half-closed, already blackening, Mimi wobbled up the steps, then sat and put her arms around both of them. "Help's coming."

Over Adrian's head, Mimi mouthed two words. *He's dead.*

Adrian would always remember the pain, and the quiet blue eyes of the paramedic who stabilized the greenstick fracture in her wrist. He had a quiet voice, too, when he shined a little light in her eyes, when he asked her how many fingers he held up.

She'd remember the policemen, the first ones who came after the sirens stopped screaming. The ones in the dark blue uniforms.

But most of it, even as it happened, seemed blurry and distant.

They huddled in the second-floor sitting room with its view of the back courtyard and its little koi pond. Mostly the police in the uniforms talked to her mother because they took Mimi to the hospital.

Her mother told them the man's name, Jonathan Bennett, and how he taught English literature at Georgetown University. Or did, when she knew him.

Her mother said what happened, or started to.

Then a man and a woman came in. The man was really tall and wore a brown tie. His skin was a darker brown, and his teeth really white. The woman had red hair cut short, and freckles all over her face.

They had badges like on TV shows.

"Ms. Rizzo, I'm Detective Riley, and this is my partner, Detective Cannon." The woman hooked her badge back on her belt. "We know this is difficult, but we need to ask you and your daughter some questions."

Then she smiled at Adrian. "It's Adrian, right?"

When Adrian nodded, Riley looked back at Lina. "Is it all right if Adrian shows me her room, if she and I talk there while you talk to Detective Cannon?"

"Will it be quicker that way? They took my friend—my daughter's nanny—to the hospital. Broken nose, concussion. And Adrian has what the paramedic thinks is a greenstick fracture on her left wrist, and she hit her head."

"You look a little rough yourself," Cannon commented, and Lina shrugged. Then winced at the movement.

"Bruised ribs will heal, so will my face. He really focused on my face."

"We can have you taken to the hospital now, and talk there once you've seen a doctor."

"I'd rather go when . . . you're finished downstairs."

"Understood." Riley looked back at Adrian. "Is it okay if we talk in your room, Adrian?"

"I guess so." She got up, holding her arm in its sling close to her chest. "I won't let you take my mom to jail."

"Don't be silly, Adrian."

Ignoring her mother, Adrian stared into Riley's eyes. They were green, but lighter than her mother's. "I won't let you."

"Got it. We're just going to talk, okay? Is your room up here?"

"Two doors down on the right," Lina said. "Go on, Adrian, go with Detective Riley. Then we'll go check on Mimi. Everything's going to be fine."

Adrian led the way and Riley put her smile back on as they walked into a room done in soft pinks and spring greens. A big stuffed dog lay on the bed.

"This is a pretty great room. And really tidy."

"I had to clean it up this morning, or no going to see the cherry blossoms and get ice cream sundaes." She winced, much like Lina had. "Don't tell about the sundaes. We were supposed to get frozen yogurt."

"Our secret. Is your mom really strict about what you eat?"

"Sometimes. Mostly." Tears sparkled into her eyes. "Is Mimi going to die like the man did?"

"She got hurt, but not real bad. And I know they're taking good care of her. How about we sit here with this guy?"

Riley sat on the side of the bed, gave the big dog a pat. "What's his name?"

"He's Barkley. Harry gave him to me for Christmas. We can't have a real dog now because we live in New York and travel too much."

"He looks like a great dog. Can you tell me and Barkley what happened?"

It poured out, a flood through a break in a dam.

"The man came to the door. He kept buzzing and buzzing, so I went out to see. I'm not supposed to open the door myself, so I waited for Mimi. She came out from the kitchen and opened the door. Then she tried to shut it again, really fast, but he pushed it open, and he pushed her. He almost knocked her down."

"Did you know him?"

"Nuh-uh, but Mimi did, because she called him Jon and told him to go away. He was mad and yelling and saying bad words. I'm not supposed to say them."

"That's okay." Riley kept petting Barkley like he was a real dog. "I get the gist."

"He wanted to see my mom, but Mimi said she wasn't here even though she was. She was upstairs taking a shower. And he kept yelling, and he slapped her face. He hit her. You're not supposed to hit. Hitting somebody's wrong."

"It was wrong."

"I yelled at him to leave her alone because he had her arms, and he was hurting her. And he looked at me—he didn't see me before, but he looked at me, and it made me scared how he looked at me. But he was hurting Mimi, and I got mad. Mimi said to go upstairs, to me, I mean, but he was hurting her. Then he—he hit her with—with his fist."

Adrian made one with her good hand while tears began to slide down her cheeks. "And there was blood, and she fell, and I ran. I ran to try to get to Mom, but he caught me. He pulled my hair, he pulled it so hard, and he pulled me up the stairs like that, and I was yelling for Mom."

"You want to stop, honey? We can wait for you to tell me the rest."

"No. No. Mom ran out, and saw him. And she kept saying for him to let me go, but he wouldn't. He kept saying she'd ruined his life, with a lot of bad words. The really bad ones, and she kept saying she hadn't told, and she'd fix it, but to let me go. He was hurting me. And he called me bad names, and he—he, threw me."

"He threw you?"

"At the stairs. He threw me at the stairs, and I hit, and my wrist, it went on fire, and I hit my head, but I didn't fall down the stairs very far. Just like a couple, I guess. And my mom screamed at him, and she ran at him, and she fought with him. He hit her face, and he had his hands on her like . . ."

She mimed choking.

"I couldn't move, and he hit her face, but she hit back, she hit back hard, and she kicked him, and they kept fighting, and then . . . then he went over the railing. She pushed him to get away, to get to me. Her face had blood, and she pushed him, and he went over the railing. It was his fault."

"Okay."

"Mimi crawled up the steps while Mom got me and held me, and she said help was coming. And everybody had blood on them. Nobody ever hit me before he did. I hate he was my father."

"How do you know he was?"

"Because of what he was yelling, what he called me. I'm not stupid. And he teaches at the college where my mom went to college, and she told me she met my father in college. So." Adrian lifted her shoulders. "That's it. He hit everybody, and he smelled bad, and he tried to throw me down the stairs. He fell because he was mean."

Riley put an arm around Adrian's shoulders and thought: That sounds about right.

They kept Mimi in the hospital overnight. Lina bought hospital gift shop flowers—the best she could do—to take to her room. Adrian had the first X-ray of her life, and would earn the first cast of her life once the swelling went down.

Rather than try to complete Mimi's dinner plans, Lina ordered pizza.

God knew the kid deserved it. Just like she herself deserved a really, really big glass of wine.

She poured one, and while Adrian ate, broke her long-standing rule and poured a second.

She had a million calls to make, but they'd wait. Every goddamn thing would wait until she felt steadier.

They ate in the back courtyard with its shady trees and privacy fence. Or Adrian ate while Lina nibbled on a single slice between sips of wine.

Maybe it was a bit cool for outdoor dining, and more than a little late to have Adrian fill up on pizza, but a vicious day was a vicious day.

She hoped her daughter would sleep, but had to admit she was a little vague on the nighttime ritual. Mimi handled that.

Maybe a bubble bath—as long as she kept the temporary cast dry. The thought of the cast, and how much worse it could have been, had her longing to top off her wineglass again.

But she resisted. Lina had a good handle on self-discipline.

"How come he was my father?"

Lina looked over, saw those gold-green eyes watching her.

"Because I was once young and stupid. I'm sorry. I'd say I wish I hadn't been, but then you wouldn't be here, would you? Can't fix what used to be, only what's now and coming up."

"Was he nicer when you were young and stupid?"

Lina let out a laugh, and her ribs whined pitifully. How much, she wondered, did you tell a seven-year-old?

"I thought he was."

"Did he hit you before?"

"Once. Only once, and after that I never, ever saw him again. If a man hits you once, he's probably going to hit you again, and again."

"You said before that you loved my dad, but things didn't work out, and he didn't want us, so he didn't matter anymore."

"I thought I loved him. I should've said that. I was only twenty, Adrian. He was older, and handsome and charming and smart. A young professor. I fell in love with who I thought he was. And he didn't matter between then and now."

"Why was he so mad today?"

"Because someone, a reporter, found out, and wrote a story. I don't know how, I don't know who told him. I didn't."

"You didn't because he didn't matter."

"That's exactly right."

How much did you tell? Lina thought again. Under the circumstances, maybe all of it.

"He was married, Adrian. He had a wife, and two children. I didn't know. That is, he lied to me, and told me he was in the middle of a divorce. I believed him."

Had she? Lina wondered. So hard to remember now.

"Maybe I just wanted to, but I believed him. He had his own little apartment near the college, so I believed he was essentially single. Later I found out I wasn't the only one he lied to. When I found out the truth, I broke things off. He didn't really care."

Not fully true, she thought. Screamed, threatened, shoved.

"Then I realized I was pregnant. Later, much later than I should have realized, I felt like I had to tell him. That's when he hit me. He wasn't drunk, like today."

He'd been drinking, she thought, but not drunk. Not like today.

"I told him I didn't want or need anything from him, that I wouldn't humiliate myself by telling anyone he was the biological father. And I left."

Lina edited out the threats, the demands she get rid of it, and all the other ugliness. No point in it.

"I finished out the term, graduated, then I went home. Popi and Nonna helped me. You know the rest, how I started doing classes and videos when I was pregnant with you—for pregnant women, then after for moms and babies."

"Yoga Baby."

"Right."

"But he was always mean. Does that mean I will be, too?"

God, she sucked at this mother thing. She did her best to think what her own mother would say.

"Do you feel mean?"

"Sometimes I get mad."

"Tell me about it." But Lina smiled. "Mean's a choice, I think, and you don't choose to be mean. He was right, too, that you don't look like him. Too much Rizzo in you."

Lina reached across the table, took Adrian's good hand. Maybe it felt too much like speaking adult to adult, but it was the best she could do.

"He doesn't matter, Adrian, unless we let him matter. So we won't let him matter."

"Are you going to have to go to jail?"

Lina toasted with her wineglass. "You're not going to let them, remember?" Then she saw the quick fear, and squeezed Lina's hand. "I'm joking, just joking. No, Adrian. The police could see what happened. You told the detective the truth, right?"

"I did. I promise."

"So did I. So did Mimi. You put that out of your mind. What is going to happen is because there was this story, and then this happened, there'll be more stories. I'm going to talk to Harry soon, and he'll help me deal with that."

"Can we still go to Popi and Nonna's?"

"Yes. As soon as Mimi's better, after you get your cast, after I deal with some things, we're going there."

"Can we go soon? Really soon?"

"As soon as we can. Just a few days maybe."

"That's soon. Everything will be better there."

A long time, Lina thought, before things would be better. But she polished off her wine. "Absolutely."

NORA ROBERTS

(c) Bruce

For the latest news, exclusive extracts and unmissable competitions, visit

f /NoraRobertsJDRobb
www.fallintothestory.com